Thomas Ball

The Life of the Renowned Doctor Preston

Thomas Ball

The Life of the Renowned Doctor Preston

ISBN/EAN: 9783337416850

Printed in Europe, USA, Canada, Australia, Japan

Cover: Foto ©Raphael Reischuk / pixelio.de

More available books at **www.hansebooks.com**

THE LIFE

OF THE

RENOWNED DOCTOR PRESTON,

WRIT BY HIS PUPIL, MASTER THOMAS BALL, D.D.

MINISTER OF NORTHAMPTON,

In the Year 1628.

NOW FIRST PUBLISHED AND

EDITED BY E. W. HARCOURT, Esq., M.P.

OF NUNEHAM PARK,

OXON.

Parker and Co.

OXFORD, AND 6 SOUTHAMPTON-STREET,

STRAND, LONDON.

1885.

Introduction.

N the year 1847, when Samuel Wilberforce, then Bishop of Oxford, was visiting at Nuneham, his attention was called to a manuscript written by the celebrated John Evelyn of Wotton, being a memoir of Margaret Godolphin.

My grandfather, who was great-great-grandson of John Evelyn, entrusted the manuscript to Bishop Wilberforce for publication; and, accordingly, "The Life of Mrs. "Godolphin, by John Evelyn of "Wootton,

"Wootton, Esqr., now first pub-
"lished and edited by Samuel,
"Lord Bishop of Oxford, Chan-
"cellor of the most noble order of
"the Garter," was given to the public, through the agency of Messrs.
Pickering. The book was received
with much favour by the public,
and went through several editions.
The only matter of regret was that
the manuscript was never restored
to the Nuneham library.

There is yet another manuscript
at Nuneham, which appears to me
worthy of notice; namely, "The
"Life of the Renowned D^r. Preston,
"Master of Emanuel College in
"the University of Cambridge,
"writ by the Reverend Thomas
"Ball, Minister of Northampton."
Bishop

Bishop Wilberforce, in his introduction to the " Life of M^rs. Godolphin," says, that " her lot was cast " in the darkest age of England's " morals ; she lived in a court " where flourished in their rankest " luxuriance all the vice and little- " ness which the envy of de- " tractors without has ever loved " to impute—and at times, thank " God, with such utter falsehood— " to courts in general. In the reign " of Charles the Second that revul- " sion of feeling which affects na- " tions just as it does individuals " had plunged into dissipation all " ranks, on their escape from the " narrow austerities and gloomy " sourness of Puritanism."

The " Renowned " Dr. Preston lived

lived one hundred years before Mrs. Godolphin, in times which gave birth to that Puritanism to which Bishop Wilberforce refers. The death of the Scottish Queen and the sailing of the Spanish Armada were the stirring events which occupied the thoughts of Englishmen at the period of Preston's birth.

At the time of Elizabeth's accession to the throne, Rome claimed the allegiance of three-fourths of her subjects; but, in the few years that followed, England became firmly Protestant. Under Henry the Eighth the Romish priests were sensual and ignorant; the Protestant clergy appointed in the reign of Edward the Sixth were almost

almost worse; the days of Hooker and Herbert, however, marked a disappearance of the grosser scandals amongst ministers of religion. Elizabeth's early policy was to leave matters alone, and to trust to time to work out the ecclesiastical reforms which she favoured; but the persecuting energy that was developed towards the end of her reign effectually alienated that Romish remnant, which at one time appeared to be becoming reconciled to the national Church.

The accession of James the First raised the hopes of the Roman party, and apparently with good foundation, for at the commencement of his reign the persecutions were relaxed; the truce, however, was

was of short duration. The king himself was too narrow-minded to take a statesman-like view of either civil or religious affairs, and his natural abilities, which were great, were cramped in their nature. His conceits and humours had, at times, a certain pleasant savour about them, as is somewhat illustrated in the following pages ; but he was entirely wanting in that strength of character which, emboldened by its own conscious rectitude and by a charitable respect for a like recti-tude in others, could alone have given him any hold on the affec-tions of the people over whom he was called upon to reign.

A new conception of social equa-lity (a matter of religion amongst the

the Puritans) was gradually dis-
placing the over-weening sense of
social distinction which had charac-
terized former history. The jea-
lousy with which any indication of
this new temper was met by those
in authority, and the unwise means
taken to repress it, were amongst
the chief causes of the troubles that
followed. Into a consideration of
those troubles it is needless now
to enter; suffice it to say that the
excesses to which they led on the
one side were followed by a natural
rebound on the other.

In such trying times were Doctor
Preston's lines cast. Of such times
our memoir is highly illustrative.
Fortunate is it for us that we
are able to look upon the scenes
here

here depicted merely as matters of curiosity and wonder.

I have followed the example of the Bishop of Oxford in leaving both the orthography and the phraseology of the manuscript in their original state, wherever they were not unintelligible. Indeed, the quaint, crisp phrases which prevail would have lost their charm if any attempt had been made to translate them.

In "The History of the Wor-"thies of England, endeavoured "by Thomas Fuller, D.D., 1662," we find the following notice of John Preston :—

" Before he commenced Master "of

"of Arts he was so far from emi-
"nency as but a little above con-
"tempt; thus the most gracious
"wines are the most muddy before
"they are fine. Soon after, his
"skill in philosophy rendered him
"to the general respect of the Uni-
"versity.

"He was the greatest pupil-
"monger in England in man's me-
"mory, having sixteen fellow-com-
"moners (most heirs to fair estates),
"admitted in one year in Queen's
"Colledge, and provided convenient
"accommodations for them. As
"William, the popular Earl of Nas-
"sau, was said to have won a sub-
"ject from the King of Spain to his
"own party every time he put off his
"hat, so was it commonly said in
"the

" the Colledge that every time when
" Master Preston plucked off his
" hat to D^r. Davenant, the Colledge
" Master, he gained a chamber
" or study for one of his pupils.
" Amongst whom, one Chambers,
" a Londoner (who dyed very
" young), was very eminent for his
" learning.

" Being chosen Master of Ema-
" nuel Colledge he removed thither
" with most of his pupills, and I
" remember, when it was much ad-
" mired where all these should find
" lodgings in that Colledge, which
" was so full already, Oh! said
" one, Master Preston will carry
" Chambers along with him.

" The party called Puritan being
" then

"then most active in Parliament,
"and D^r. Preston most powerful
"with them, the Duke * rather used
"then loved him to work that party
"to his complyance. Some thought
"the Doctor was unwilling to do
"it, others thought he was unable,
"that party being so diffusive, and
"then in their designs (as since
"in their practises) divided. How-
"ever, whilst any hope, none but
"D^r. Preston with the Duke, set
"by and extolled; and, afterwards,
"set by and neglected, when found
"useless to the intended purpose.
"In a word, my worthy friend fitly
"calls him the Court Comet, blaz-
"ing for a time and faiding soon
"afterwards.

---

* The Duke of Buckingham.

"He

"He was a perfect politician,
"and used (lapwing like) to flutter
"most on that place which was
"furthest from his eggs; exact at
"that concealing of his intentions,
"with that simulation which some
"make to lye in the marches of
"things lawfull and unlawfull. He
"had perfect command of his pas-
"sion, with the Caspian Sea never
"ebbing nor flowing; and would
"not alter his compos'd pase for
"all the whipping which satyrical
"wits bestowed upon him. He
"never had wife or cure of souls;
"and, leaving a plentifull, yet no
"envidious estate, died Anno Do-
"mini, 1628, July 20."

For a couple of centuries the
manuscript lives of Mrs. Godolphin
and

and of the "Renowned D^r. Preston," had lain side by side amongst the Nuneham Papers.

Widely different indeed was the stern Puritan from the delicate Saint, but there are good lessons to be learnt from the lives of each ; and I take it that this one lesson alone would suffice to warrant the printing of the manuscripts, namely, that, whether in the rougher roads of a professional career, or in the softer paths of a courtly and domestic life, it is very possible to keep "unspotted from the world."

E. W. H.

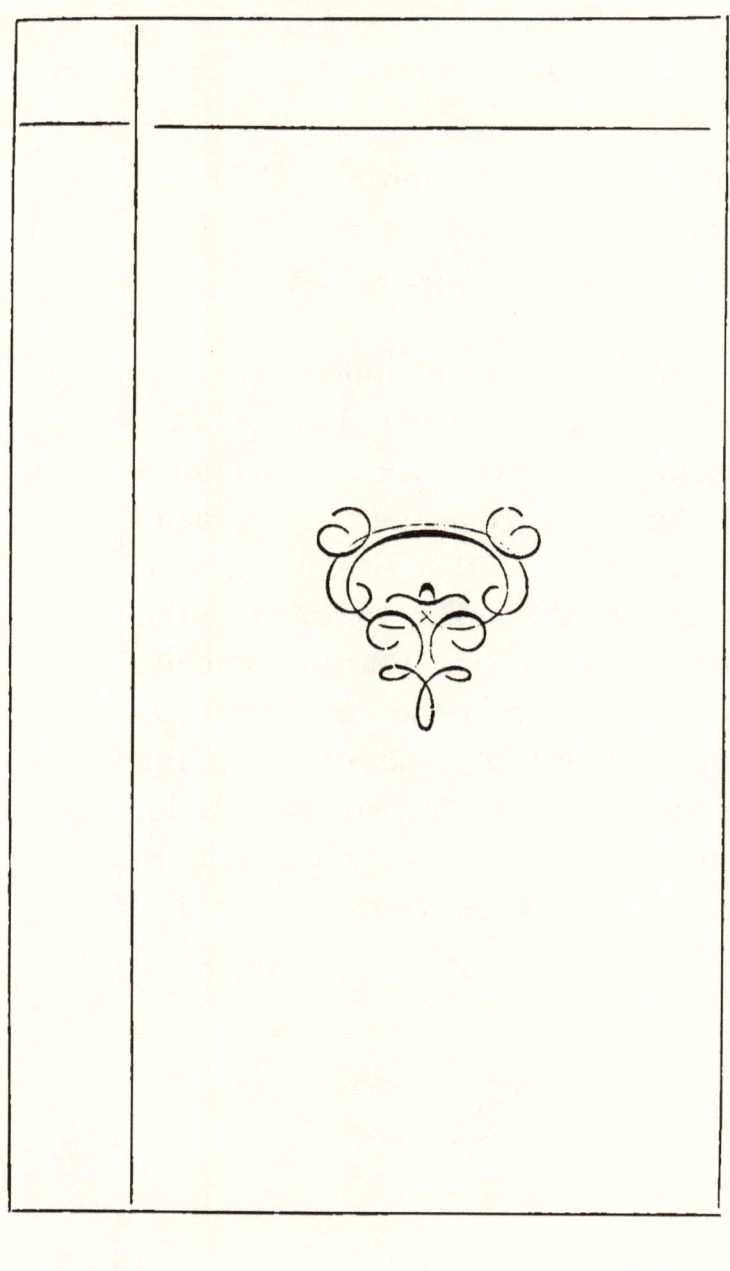

The Life of Doct^r Preston

who dyed

ANNO CHRISTI. 1628.

 OHN PRESTON, the son of Thomas & Alice Preston, was borne at Heyford, in Northamptonshire ; a towne divided by a little river into y^e Upper and Lower Heyfords, and is in the Maps oft writ in ye plural number. It is a Rectory, and hath a faire church in the Lower Heyford, but yet stands in divers parrishes.

That farme where M^r. Thomas Preston lived is in Bugbrooke parrish, where they

they buried & baptized. Heere was John the son of Thomas Preston baptized Octob 27th 1587. Yet was descended from that family of the Prestons that lived at Preston in Lancashire, from whence his great grand-father removed, upon occasion of a fatall quarrel wth one M^{r}. Bradshaw a neighbour - gentleman, whom in his owne defence he slew, & satisfied the law, & was acquitted for it; but not the kindred of the person killed, who wayted an oppᵗunity of revenge, as the manner of those Northern Countryes then was.

It fell out not long after, that M^{r}. Bradshaw's next brother meets M^{r}. Preston neare the place where he had slayne his brother, & told him that he should doe as much for him, or he would revenge his blood; M^{r}. Preston told him that he had slaine his brother in his owne defence, & against his will; that he bore no evil mynde unto them,

&

& therefore desired him he would forbeare; but when nothing would prevaile they fought, & Bradshaw fell againe. At wch M^r. Preston was greatly troubled and grieved, for he saw that a fire was kindled that would not easily be quenched; and therefore resolved that he would leave that fatall country, though he was a gentleman of a very faire Estate. So walking one day very pensive in Westminster Hall, one M^r. Morgan of Heyford, wth whom he was acquainted, came unto him & demanded why he was so sad, to whom for answer he related ye former story.

M^r. Morgan knowing him to be a very gallant man, was very sensible of his estate, & told him that if he would goe wth him to Heyford, he should have a good farme to live in for ye present and what accomodation he could afforde him. M^r. Preston thanked him, and after some consideration accepted his offer;

offer ; and so M^r. Preston of Preston in
Lancashire became a kind farmer in
Northamptonshire, where he afterwards
lived & dyed and his son succeeded him,
and so it came unto Thomas Preston as
I have sayd.

His mother's name before she marryed was Marsh, who had an Unkle by
the mother's side whose name was Cras-
well, a man of good estate & Esteeme
in Northampton, where he lived and
had been severall tymes Mayor. This
Unkle being rich and having no childe,
was very carefull of her, & tooke this
son when young to himselfe, and sent
him to the Free Schoole in Northampton ; where he was a Schollar under y^e
Goverment of M^r. Sanderson then Master of the Schoole, & after under M^r.
Wastell who succeeded him ; wth whom
remayning some tyme, his Unkle was
p̄swaded to remove him into Bedfordshire, unto one M^r. Guest, who had
some

some tyme taught a private schoole in Northampton, & was accounted a better teacher of ye Greeke tongue; from whence, after he had prosecuted his studies in ye Greeke, he was sent to Cambridge, & admitted of King's Colledge under the tuition of M^r. Busse, one of the Fellows, Anno Domini 1604.

Here he did as young schollars used to doe, that is applyed himself to the Genius of the College, & that was musique; and finding that the theory was shorte and soone atteyned, he made account ye practise would also be so; and accordingly adventured upon the Lute, the hardest instrument; but heere he found though theory was shorte, art was long; & so as unwilling to attend it, he used to say whilst fingering his lute, " Quantum hoc tempore Legi potuit;" and while his fingers were thus foundred on the Lute, it fell out that his Tutor M^r. Busse was chosen Master of the Schole

Schole at Eaton, & so removed from yᵉ
Colledge, about two yeares after he was
admitted; but coming not from Eaton
but from another, he could not be of yᵉ
foundation, and therefore uncapable of
those Preferments in yᵉ College that were
most worth, and so yᵉ sooner p̄swaded
to remove ; this he did unto Queen's
College, where he was received & admitted under yᵉ tuition of Mʳ. Oliver
Bowles, one of yᵉ fellows of that House,
a very holy & learned man, a noted &
carefull Tutor ; under his government
he setled to his booke, & left his
musique, by whose conduct & directions
he grew in knowledge, and was improved unto very thriving undertakings
in his studies.

It is not nothing to be well descended,
"fortes creantur fortibus et bonis." Sheep
& cattle bred in Lancashire, or on the
Peake Hills, & after driven into Northamptonshire & planted there, produce

a

a very gallant race; These Prestons,
though removed from their native soyle
& much impaired in their revenue, re-
teined yet yᵉ Garb and mettal of their
Ancestors; they carried themselves, &
were accounted Gentlemen. Something
there was in this young Preston's Spirit
that was not vulgar; I have seen in a
booke of his, under his owne hand when
younge, such sparklings of aspiring in-
genuity as argued in him something
that was not common.

He was as yet but junior Sophister,
yet looked high & grew acquainted wᵗʰ
those that were Gentile, & fancied State
affairs, and Courtship, & that had desires or dispositions to be secretaries or
agents in Princes' Courtes; he now
thought it below him to be a minister,
& held the study of Divinity to be a
kind of honest silliness; he accordingly got acquainted wᵗʰ a merchant,
by whose means he did procure that
he

His ambi-
tion to be
a courtier,
and under-
valluing
the High-
est im-
ployment
of yᵉ min-
istry.

he should live in Paris and learn ye language & garb of France, & another in recompense should be exchandged to learne the mode & English tongue. M^r. Craswel, his Unkle at Northampton was by this tyme dead, and had bequeathed certeine Lands in that Towne to him after his wive's decease ; these Lands he sells to put himselfe into a posture fit for that designe ; But heere now he began to finde that he reckoned without his host ; and that he should have said as the Apostle, James, 4—15. " If the Lord will I shall live, & doe this or that ;" for the merchant dyes before the exchandge could be accomplished, & so those blooming hopes, that had thus long held up his imagination, died wth the merchant.

He was of an able, firme, well tempered constitution, browne, comely vissadge, vigorous and vived eye, but somewhat enclyning to that kinde of melancholly

melancholly that ariseth from a dust
& parched choller, wᶜʰ now began a
little to be discovered in him ; for
being thus mated in his first designe,
he grew discouraged, went not so much
abroade amongst yᵉ gallants, but struck
sayle to fortune, & retyred ; yet his
apetite was rather dammed up than
dryed ; for after a very little pause, &
boyling over of his sullenness, he began
again to steere the same course, although by more certaine & domesticque
mediums, and if he must be shut up &
confined to the Muses, resolves to be no
ordinary servant to them.

His genius led him unto Naturall
Philosophy, wᶜʰ by that tyme was become his propp taske, wᶜʰ he undertooke not as boyes use to doe, to serve
their present use, but wᵗʰ devotion resolves to leave no secret unattempted ;
Adoreth Aristotle as his tutelary saint,
and had a happiness usually to enter
when

when others stuck, and what was diffi-
cult to others he made little of.

No darke untrodden path in all his
physicks & metaphysicks but he was
perfect in it ; & so drowned & devoted
was he, that he seldome or never could
be seene abroad, to the wonder &
amazement of his former brave com-
panions, so that no tyme passed "sine
Linea," no not that betweene the ringing
& tolling of the Bell to meales. And
for his sleepe, he would let the bed
cloathes hang downe, that in the night
they might fall off, & so the cold
awaken him ; In so much that his tutor was constreyned to reade unto him
moderation ; and to tell him that as
there might be intemperance in meates
& drinkes, so also there might be in
studies ; but the evill of it, as yet he
felt not ; the sweet & ye good he did,
who came off wth great honour and applause in all his acts, and was admired
in

in yᵉ Regent House when he sate for
his degree, both by yᵉ Posers & all
the Masters that examined him, and
from that tyme much observed in yᵉ
University.

About this tyme his tutor Mʳ. Bowles
was called to yᵉ Rectory of Sutton in
Bedfordshire, & so left yᵉ college, and
another of yᵉ fellows, then Master,
afterwards Doctor Potter, became his
Tutor, a very learned man & great
philosopher, who never went about to
diswade him from his studies, but gave
him all assistance & encouragement.
The yeare following it came unto his
tutor to be Head Lecturer in the College, and Sʳ. Preston being to probleme
in the Chappel, made such an accu-
rate & strong position, & answered so
understandingly, that his Tutor bor-
rowed his position of him when he had
done, to looke & p̅u̅se ; & finding it
elaborate, resolved to make more use of
it,

it, then ever his pupil did intend.   The
master of ye college at that tyme was
Doctor Tyndal, who was also Deane of
Ely, & resided for the most p̄te there;
to whom the Tutor went, & carried his
position wth him ; wch he shewed to y^e
Master and acquainted him wth what he
had observed, that he was a youth of
great p̄tes and worth, & deserved some
encouragement ; the Master was an
honest gallant man & loved a schollar,
& glad of an opertunity to show it, &
so bids his tutor to send S^r. Preston
over to him to Ely, assuring him that
he should not want what was in him to
doe him good, & bade him hold on, for
he would take care of him.

Soon after which there being an
election in ye College, he was chosen
fellow by unanimous consent of Master & fellows ; when his tutor M^r.
Porter brought him word of it, as he
was at study not thinking of it, & told
him

him he must come downe presently
into ye Chappel to be admitted ; And
accordingly was admitted fellow of
Queen's College, in Cambridge, 1609,
that is, five yeares after his first admis-
sion into ye University. He was not
so much mouved at it as young students use to be, because he still looked
at higher thinges, & had not quit in his
retired thoughts his first designe of
being some body at Court, to wch he
thought this honour might be a barr.
This curtesy was "non compos" to him,
yet it was not manners to be discontent,
but attend what should ensue.

He was by this time growne a master
in Philosophy, had waded far in Aristotle,
& met wth few that were able to encoun-
ter him; and therefore resolves to goe another while to schoole to Hypocrates &
Galen, & so verify what is so often said,
" Ubi desinit Philosophus, incipit medi-
cus." He had a very penetrating wit,
and

and exact judgement to conjecture of effects in causes, & prognostical events, & being skilfull in philosophy before, soone made the theory his owne, but because "Perfectio scientiarum est in summitate," the life & vigour of a science is in the Practice, he resolves to make enquiry after that ; Bookes makes not men practitioners in any art, "Memo ex libris evasit artifex."

He retires to a friend of his in Kent, who was very famous for his practice, where he earnestly attended, & waited on ye trade & way of knowing simples, & compounding medicines, wherein he atteyned to that sufficiency, that had divinity failed, he might have been another D^r. Butler ; yet what he had was not in vaine, for when any of his pupils were not well, though he sent them always to physitians, yet himselfe p̄used, & many times corrected their prescriptions. It was not easy to allay his

eager

eager and unsatisfied apetite wth any one art, Eccles. 5—10. " He that loveth silver shall not be satisfied wth it," "Crescit amor Nummi, quantum ipsa pecunia crescit," the more you put into the soule ye wider presently it retcheth; He thought he could not be a good physician that could not reade ye powers of herbs & plants in stars & planets; Therefore he acquainted himself with Ptolomy, & other authours in Astrology, and other curious arts & calculations, as they are called. Acts 19. 19. that he might be able not only to study bookes, but men, & to reade men's fortunes in ye Heavenly bodyes.

But he could not, nor did reade his owne ; there was a Southsayer that told Agathocles he should be slaine the next month ; who asked how long he thought he should live after him ? he answered many yeares; he told him he would prove one of ye two false, & leave the other

other to the issue; & so commanded for to hange him presently. M^r. Preston was very busy amonge ye Howses of ye planets, but saw not there his owne domestick doome, nor what his Maker had determined concerning him; for, as he was in the Cælestial contemplations, it fell out that M^r. Cotton then fellow of Emanuel College preached in S^t. Marye's; where, M^r. Preston hearing him, was set about another Exercise, constreyned from his contemplations in Astrology to looke into himself, & consider what might possibly befall him.

Mr. Preston converted by Mr. Cotton's Sermon.

It was his manner, as of other students, when they come home from ye sermons at S^t. Marye's to run unto their studies presently, or what was worse; but this young student was forced to retire & ruminate. The sermon had bereaved him of two beloved notions; one was his low opinion of the ministry & preaching; for he saw an over-ruling gravity

gravity and Majesty in that sermon, that he thought had bin impossible to pulpits.

I have heard it often in ye college that he tooke away sixteene answers in a probleme in the Chappel, but heere was one he knew not how to take away. "Sed hæret lateri Lethalis arundo." No cunning in philosophy or skill in physick would suffice to heale this wound. Another (beloved notion he was bereaved of) was his great opinion of & ambition after State Imployments; for these were higher thinges y^t now were offered to him; concernements of Eternal Influence, wch nothing could divert that he had studied hitherto.

There have been divers eminent & great physicians that began in medling wth their owne infirmities. Self love rides always on the forehorss. His owne accounts, and aking conscience, set Luther

first

first upon yᵉ study of Divinity. Mʳ. Preston, after this affront & baffle in yᵉ Pulpit, wanted ease; &, when he could not finde it in his other bookes & studies, begins a little to looke into yᵉ Bible, & to consider of yᵉ study of Divinity.

In the prosecution of his study in Philosophy, he found many of the schoolemen quoted, & so was willing to looke a little into them, and, finding those he lighted on pithy & sententious, went on.

It gave him ease that he was now a student in Divinity, and had left Al-bumaser, & Guido, & such high flowne speculations; yet it pleased him for to see & finde his master Aristotle so often quoted, & in such request amonge them; and thought, if that were to be a Preacher, he might adventure well enough on it; & so was drawne

on

on very farr into ye study of ye schoolemen. I have heard him say, there was
nothing that ever Scotus or Occham
wrote, but he had weighed & examined; he delighted much to reade
them in the first & oldest editions that
could be got; I have still a Scotus, in
a very old print & a paper not inferiour
to parchment, that hath his hand & notes
upon it throughout; Yet he continued
longer in Aquinas, whose summes he
would sometimes read as the Barber
cut his haire, and when any fell upon
the place he read, he would not lay
downe his booke but blow it off; and
in this tune he continued, untill a
rumour came into ye university that ye
King would shortly come to visit them.

King James was happier in his educa-
tion then his Mother would have had
him; it pleased God to breede a Bu-
chanon on purpose to guide his younger
yeares; and, by that tyme he was ripe,
Scotland

Scotland was growne acquainted wth Geneve, & the King no stranger unto M^r. Calvin's way. The newes awakened all ye University, & there were few but promised themselves some good from this faire Gale ; that, seeing promotion came neither from ye East, nor West, nor from the South, Psal. 75. 6, it must and would come from the North ; and the Proverb be inverted, and be " Omne bonum ab Aquilone."

Doctor Harsnet, master of Pembrooke Hall, was then Vice Chancelor, a prudent well advised Governour, who, knowing well ye critical and able apprehension of ye king, was very carefull and sollicitous to pitch upon ye ablest in every faculty for actors in that solemne enterteyn- ment, and himself made choyce of M^r. Preston to answer the Philosophy Act, and sent unto him to provide himself. He was ambitious enough by nature, and had this newes come a little sooner, nothing

nothing had bin more suitable to his inclynation and designe, but now the gentleman was Planet struck, growne dull & Phligmatique, M^r. Cotton's sermon had so invaded him, that Kings and Courts were no such great thinges to him, especially when he understood y^t another was resolved on for answerer.

Doctor Wren was then a very pregnant Schollar in Pembrooke Hall, and also chapline to Bishop Andrews, and thought fit to be imployed in this Commencement service, yet was not willing to have any other place but answerer. The Vice Chancelor urged his promise and engagement to M^r. Preston, and his opinion of his great abillity ; but nothing would serve, the Vice Chancelor's College and the Bishop's Chaplin must have precedency, wch he most seriously excused to M^r. Preston, & endeavoured to reconcile him to the first Opponent's place, wch he declyned

The Vice Chancelor of Cambridge, Doct^r Harsnet, appoints Mr. Preston to dispute in the phylosophy Act before King James.

declyned as being too obnoxious to the Answerer, who is indeed the Lord and Ruler of the Act; but there was no removing now, and so he goes about it wth much unwillingness, being rather driven than drawne unto it.

His great and first care was to bring his argument to a head, w^thout affronte or Interruptions from the Answerer; and so made all his major propositions plausible and firme, that his adversary might neither be willing, nor able, to enter there, and the minor still backt by other syllogismes; & so the Argument went on unto Issue; wch fell out well for M^r. Preston; for, in disputations of consequence, the Answerers are many times so fearfull of y^e. event that they Slur & trouble ye opponents all they can and deny things evident; wch had bin the case in all former Acts; There was such wrangling about their Syllogismes that sullyed and clouded the

the debates extreamely, and put the King's Acumen into Streights.

But when M^r. Preston still cleared his way, and nothing was denied, but what was ready to be proved, the King was greatly satisfied, & gave good heede, wch he might well doe, because the question was tempered & fitted to his content: namely whether Dogs could make syllogismes*. The opponent urged that they could; an Ethymeme (said he), is a lawfull & reall syllogisme, but dogs can make them; he instanced in a Hound, who hath ye major proposition in his minde, namely, the hare is gone either this way, or that way, smells out the minor wth his nose, namely, she is not gone that way, & follows the conclusion, "Ergo," this way, wth open mouth.

The instance suited wth ye Auditory and was applauded, and put the Answerer to his distinctions, that dogs

* Note.—The King was a great Huntsman.

might

might have sagacity, but not sapience, in thinges especially of Prey, and that did not concerne their belly, might be " nasutuli" but not " Logici," had much in their mouths, little in their myndes, unless it had relation to their mouths, that their lips were larger than their understandings; which the opponent still endeavoured to evade with another syllogisme, & put the dogs upon a fresh scent. The Moderator, Doctor Reade, began to be afraid, and to think how troublesome a pack of hounds well followed and applauded at last might prove; and so came in unto the Answerer's Ayd, and told the Opponent that his dogs he beleeved were very weary, and desired him to take them off; and when the Opponent would not yeild, but hallowed still and put them on, he interposed his authority & silenced him.

The King, in his conceit, was all this while

while upon New Market Heath, & liked the sport; and, therefore, stands up and tells the Moderator plainly he was not satisfied in all that had bin answered, but did beleeve a hound had more in him than was imagined. I had myself (said he) a dog that stragling farr from all his fellows had light upon a very fresh scent, but considering he was all alone and had none to second and assist him in it, observes the place & goes away to his fellows, and by such yelling argu-ments as they best understand, pre-vayled wᵗʰ a p̄ty of them to goe along wᵗʰ him, and, bringing them to the place, p̄sued it into an open view. Now the King desired for to know how this could be contrived and carried on without an exercise of understand-ing, or what the Moderatour could have done in that case better, & de-sired him that either he would thinke better of his dogs or not so highly of himselfe !

The

The Opponent also desired leave to p̄sue the King's game, wch he had started to an issue; But the Answerer protested that His Majesties dogs were always to be excepted, who hunted not by com̄on law but by prerogative; but the Moderatour fearing the King might let loose another of his hounds, and make more worke, applyes himself wth all submissive devotion to the King, acknowledged his dogs were able to outdoe him, besought His Majesty to beleeve he had ye better, that he would consider how his illustrious influence had already ripened & concocted all their arguments & Understandings; that, whereas in ye morning the Reverend and Grave Divines could not make syllogismes, the Lawyers could not, nor the Physicians, now every dog could, especially His Majesties!

All men acknowledged it was a good bit to stop with, it was growne late, and

so

so the congregation was remouved unto the Regent Howse, and the King went off well pleased wth ye business ; the other acts were easily forgotten, but the discourse and logicke of the dogs was fresh in mouth and memory, & the Philosophy Act applauded universally ; the King commended all the Actors, but above all the Opponent. It was easy to discerne that ye King's hound had opened a way for M^r. Preston at ye Court if he were willing ; Yea, many of the great ones put him in mynde, and promised all assistance and encouragement. Sr Fulke Grevil, afterwards Lord Brook, was greatly taken wth him, &, after many demonstrations of his reall love, setled at last a stypend on him of fifty pounds p̄ annum, and was his friend until his last hower.

The King comends all the scholars who disputed in the Phylosophy Act, but especially M^r. Preston.

But his ambition after courtship was well allayed, so as he did not ravenously p̄sue it, being now resolved to be a minister ;

nister ; he fell to the study of moderne writers, especially M^r. Calvin, whose very style & language much affected him. The Courtiers wondred he did not bite ; because as it's said Prov. 16.15. "In the light of the King's countenance is life, and his favour is as the cloud of the latter raine ;" that a young man should not be ambitious, and a good eye not see, they did not understand ; & they began now to be a little jealous of him.

The Court jealous of Mr. Preston for not seeking preferment, when invited to it.

He was reserved naturally, and could keepe councell, so that few knew how M^r. Cotton's sermon had affected & wrought upon him ; this not sayling when the wynd blew, begat suspition ; some judged he was modest & wanted oppᵗunity to bring him on, some that he was melancholly, & so neglected what was propp̄ for him to intend, some thought him busy and intent upon his pupils who now began to come from all pts ; but the Polititians assured themselves

selves it was some inclination to puritanisme, a name now odious at Courte,
for it could not be, said they, that he
should let so faire an o͞pptunity miscarry, if he had not something else
in veiu.

Kings think themselves extreamely
undervallued, if a word be not enough.
Cardinal Poole being chosen Pope at
midnight by the conclave, & sent unto
to come & be admitted, desired it might
be let alone untill yᵉ morning, because
it was not a worke of Darkness, an
honnest Argument, but not Italian
enough. " Quis nisi mentis inops." So
they went back & chose another. When
Balaam came not at the first call, see
how Balack reasons. Numb. 22. 37.
"Am I not able indeed to promote
thee to honour ?"

But Mʳ. Preston indeed had another
King in his thoughts, &, having found
                                    treasure

treasure in the field, parts wth all for that. Mat. 13. 44. A purchass is not worth the having that hath not some convenience annexed, or may not some way be improved. God was a greater good than man. Heaven than Earth, a Crowne of Glory than a Crowne of Gold. So this neglect & sefe deniall was well interpreted by good men, and the opinion that he affected Puritans, which blasted him at Court, begun to blazon him at home, and worke a reputation, that to him was more acceptable.

Many thought him meete to be trusted wth the care of youth and had their eyes upon him for their sons or friends. M^r. Morgan of Heyford had been some tyme dead, and left his son & heyre an orphan in trust with some that were his kinsmen and like to manadge his estate to most advantage ; who, when sent to the University,

sity, was bequeathed to M^r. Preston's care; not only for the relation he had to Heyford, his native Towne, and that familly, but also that, by that means, the young gentleman might be preserved from the influence of his other friends, who were many of them Popish!

King James had bin so well pleased at the Commencement held before him lately, that he resolves upon another visit; The Heads agree to enterteine him wth a comedy. There was one Fuggles of Clare Hall, that had made a jeering comedy against ye Lawyers, called "Ignoramus;" this was resolved on to be acted before the King, and great care was taken to accomodate all parts, wth Actors answerable.

M^r. Morgan was a comely modest gentleman, and was supposed would well become a woman's dress, and accordingly his Tutor M^r. Preston sent to,
                                                    that

that he would admit and give all encouragement to the Service. He liked
not the notion, nor could believe his
friends intended he should be a Player,
& so desired to be excused ; But the
Guardians were not so exact & scru-
pulous, but thought if he played this
game well, he might winne more than
could be hoped for elsewhere ; and so M^r.
Morgan was allowed by his Guardians
to act his part, and afterwards removed
unto Oxford, & suffer'd to play what
part he would, and so relapsed to
Popery, wch hath proved fatall to him
and his.

Heere was matter for M^r. Preston's
back friends to argue he was no courtier, that would deny so small a curtesy to those that had so freely offered
him greater ; it was resented wth a kind
of angry indignation that their offers
had so little influence upon him, and
some watched an oppᵗunity to make
him

him sensible of this neglect; there is no such solœcisme at Court as independency, "si non vis ut per illos tibi benè sit, efficient ut sit male." But Mr. Preston by this tyme had cast up all accounts, & resolved to stand to his bargaine whatsoever it cost him; Only he thought if he must be a Puritan, & bid farewell to all carnall & Court designes, he would not be one of the Lower Rank, but would get places if he could. "Mediocribus esse Poetis, non Dij, non homines, non columnæ." That counsell of the wise man, Eccles. 9. 10. "whatsoever thy hand findeth to doe, doe it wth all thy might," he always practised, & what is comonly said was true in him, "in magnis ingeniis nihil mediocre."

This faithfulness to Mr. Morgan (attended wth so great a shadow unto himselfe) encreased his reputation in ye country, so that now he was accounted ye only tutor; and, being carefull to reade

reade unto them & direct their studyes, he found himselfe much abridged of his owne tyme, & was constreyned to take up tyme that should have bin bestowed on his body ; he also grew acquainted now wth many eminent & Godly ministers, as M^r. Dod and M^r. Hindersham, who would come often to his chamber, and he was so hardened in his way, that he would get them many times to goe to prayer with his pupils, a boldness not adventured on by any other ; but by these labours his able body was debilitated.

It was a great Oratour that said, " At first, said he, I would not pleade, at last I could not." M^r. Preston in his youth would not sleepe, but let ye bed cloathes hang downe so as to awaken him ; now he could not, but about midnight still awaked & slept no more : whereby in tyme his body languished, and could not answer as formerly.

M^r.

Mr. Butler of Clare Hall was then the Oracle in physick, to him he goes, & declares his condition, who, after some questions, bade him take tobacco, & so leaves him ; he knew that Butler was odd & humerous, & thought he might give him this advice to try him, and therefore resolved to wayt awhile before he medled wth so unusuall a medicine, which Hypocrates & Galen had never prescribed to any of their patients, and was at that tyme not so comon nor of good report ; but his want of rest continuing, & his appetite unto his booke encreasing, he retornes to Mr. Butler as a stranger, and propounds the case againe. Master Butler gives ye same advice, and being satisfied that he was serious now, he began to take it, and found that this hot copious fume ascending did draw those crudityes from the stomach's mouth yt hindered concoction of his meate, and vapours from it that occasion sleepe, and so restored his rest,

&

& that in tyme his strength ; and so he went on in his worke untill D^r. Tyndall, M^{er} of the College, dyed.

He was an old man, and that prefer-ment of the mastership of Queene's Colledge, more accounted of than now it is ; there were many that had their eyes upon it, but D^r. Mon-taine especially, who was often heard to profess he would rather be Mas-ter of that college than Deane of Westminster.

But M^r. Preston had another in his eye, D^r. Davenant, a gentleman well descend-ed, and was a Fellow-comoner when un-dergraduat, but very painfull and of great capacity, & grew accordingly in learning & reputation, & for his worth & p̄ts was already chosen Margret Professor, & read in the schools wth much applause those excellent lectures upon the Colos-sians

sians wch now are printed; him M^r.
Preston pitched upon, but knew it must
be carryed very privately; for the
Montaine was already growne to some
bigness, was one of p̄ts, & first observed
in acting "Miles Gloriosus" in the college, and had bin Chaplin to the Earle of
Essex, but like the Heliotrope or flower
of ye sun, did now adore Sr Robert Carr,
already Viscount Rochester, the only
favorite. When it was agreed amonge
the Persians that he should reigne whose
horss first saw the rising sun & neighed
at it, one turned his horsses head towards the Montaines, beleeving that y^e
sun would first arise there; but it fell
not out so heere.

M^r. Preston having layd his plot be-
forehand, & scene what Montaine was
in his way, had taken care that word
should be daily brought him how ye old
doctor did; and when he found him ir-
recoverable, layd horsses & all thinges
ready

ready, & upon notice of his being dead, goes presently & was at London & in Whitehall before any light appeared on the Montaine Topp. The Court was quiet, & he had some friends there, his business was only to get a free election, wch he made meanes to procure; yet knowing also wth whom he had to doe, makes some addresses unto Viscount Rochester in ye behalfe of D^r. Davenant, who, being unacquainted wth his chaplin's appetite to that p̄ticcular, was faire and willing to befriend a learned enterprise. So M^r. Preston retorned unto ye College before ye Master's death was much took notice of, and assembling D^r. Davenant's friends, acquaints them wth what had passed at Court; and so they went imediately to Election, wch was easily and fairely carryed for D^r. Davenant, who, being called, was admitted presently.

But when D^r. Montaine understood that

that Dr. Tyndal was dead, he sends & goes to Court & College for to make friends ; but alass! the game was played, and he shut out. Never did Ætna or Vesuvius more fume, but there was no care, only he threatens & takes on against ye Actors, but they were innocent, & not obnoxious. This Dr. had made great promises, & gave a very goodly peece of plate into ye College, wth this inscription, " sic incipio," but now he vowed it should be " sic desino." However the college for the present was well assayd, & grew in Reputation very much, and, because they wanted roome to enterteyne the numbers that flocked to them, they built that goodly fabrick that conteyns many faire lodgings both for fellows & scholars, towards King's College.

It was not long before it came to Mr. Preston's course to be Deane and Catechist, wch he resolved to improve by
going

going through a body of Divinity, that might be a guide to the scholars in their studies of Divinity ; for it was not his opinion that others should do as he had done, that is p̅u̅se the shoolemen first, and then come to yᵉ moderne writers ; but first reade Summes and Systemes in Divinity, so as to settle their judgements, & then to reade Fathers & scholemen, or what they had a mynde to. This being knowne, & some honnest townsmen hearing him at first by chance, there came the next day very many for to heare him, & yᵉ next day more both townsmen and scholars from other colleges, so that the outward chapple would be often full before the fellows came.

Master Preston was of a very meek & quiet spirit, never resented injuries, nor provoked any unto averseness, yet had some enimyes, " Si injuria multos tibi fecit Inimicos faciet vidia multos."

What

What had Paul done, Acts 13. 45. for
to deserve so sharpe an opposition? but
envy moved them. There had bin other
Deanes and Catechists before this
gentleman, yet no such crowding.
Complaint was made to the Vice Chancelor of this unusual kind of Catechising;
it was assured that not only townsmen
& scholars mingled, but other colleges
intruded also; that the fellows, for the
crowd & multitude, could not get
through & come to chapple to their
places; that it was not safe for any
man to be thus adored & doted on,
unless they had a minde to cry up
Puritanisme, wch would in short tyme
pull them downe; that the Crosier
staffe would not support them longe
if such assemblyes were encouraged;
"obsta principiis sero medicina paratur,"
etc.

Upon the whole an order was agreed
on in the consistory & sent unto the
College,

College, that the scholars & Townsmen should be confined to their propp Preachers; that no stranger, neither townsmen nor scholars, should presume, on any pretence whatsoever, to come to those lectures, that were propp only to the members of the college. The Edict was observed punctually, and the Auditory by it much impaired; for had strangers still bin permitted to attend, those sermons had bin printed as well as others; for there were divers that exactly noted, & wrote out all faire, unto the tyme of this restreynt, but no one after that could goe on wth it, & so it rests; but he went on & was assiduous to the Yeare's End, & waded through it, wch was a very great helpe unto many of his pupils, who made ye greater benefit of those thinges, because they were not comon & in Print.

About that tyme the Lecture at Trinity church, & ye sermons at S^t. Andrews,

Andrews, were prohibited, & ye scholars all confined to S^t. Maryes; wch did occasion M^r. Preston to reade Divinity unto his pupils on the Lorde's dayes at three of the clock in ye after-noone, wch he often did upon the weeke dayes; but the townsmen and the scholars of other colleges who had tasted of his spirit in the chapple, endeavoured that he would doe it where they might heare. Buttolphs belongs to Queen's College, and is usually supplyed by one of that Howse, there he was willing to make tryall how it would take, and resolves the next Lord's day to preach at three of ye clock, after S^t. Marye's sermon should be ended; w^{ch}, though as supposed but little knowne, occasioned such a thronge & crowd as was incredible; men were not cloyed wth preaching then, nor waxed wanton.

There dwelt then in the p̄rish, one D^r. Newcomb, a civilian & comissary to to the Chancelor of Ely, who being in the Church & seeing ye crowd, comanded that evening prayer only should be read, but no sermon ; the minister intreated that for that tyme M^r. Preston might be allowed to preach, so did ye Earl of Lincolne & others in ye church ; but he was resolute, & because he would not be further importuned, went home with his familly, & left them to determine at their perill what they would doe. So, upon advice, it was concluded that ye sermon should goe on, & M^r. Preston preached a very holy sermon upon 2 Peter 3. 17-18. There was so much time spent in debate about it, & messages, before the comissary left the congregation, that it was too late to doe both, and, therefore, they adventured for that tyme to forbeare Comon Prayer, that so the scholars might departe and be at college Prayer.

But this instructed D^r. Newcomb in his

his complaint; the Court was then neare hand at Newmarket, thither the Comissary hastens next day, and finding the Bishop of Ely there & many other clergymen, assures them that Mr. Preston was in heart, & would quickly be in practise, a Non-Conformist, and was so followed and adored in the University, that unless some speedy course were taken wth him, they might cast their caps at all Conformity, & see their power trodden under foote; and told them gentleness was not the way, for he was cunning, & would recover all, if he were not throughly dealt with.

There was an Advocate for Mr. Preston, but the Dr. being first in his owne cause seemed just, (Prov. 17. 18.) & spake to those who were willing to beleeve. The Puritans began to be considerable, & they doubted he might come in tyme to head them. It is a great security to a man to be despised, "contempto nullus

nullus diligenter nocet." A man that
hath nothing in him, & so not owned,
may be exorbitant, as he of one in his
tyme "contemptu jam liber erat." But
David, that had a p̄ty following him,
must have an army to attend him ; and
therefore he did wisely to profess himselfe a dead dog, or a flea. 1 Sam. 24. 14.

The King was made acquainted wth
this complaint, & assured that M^r. Preston had as strong an influence into the
Puritans, as the Principle of ye Jesuits,
wch was "Aqua viva" to others ; and
therefore it behoved him to consider
what to doe. A word was enough to
a wise & jealous King, who did not
love to play an after game, and, therefore, hearde himselfe ye Doctor's information, enquires whether the Bishop's & Chancellor's jurisdiction ex-
tended to members of a College, &
finally concludes to proceed against
him by the power of the University.

A

A letter is framed at y^c tyme to D^r. Scot, Master of Clare Hall, Vice Chancellor at that tyme, and to the Heads, to call before them M^r. Preston, to give a strict account of ye notorious disobedience unto the Comisary; he answers mildly that he was not guilty; refers himself to the Auditory that Evening prayer was omitted because the schollars might dep^{te} in due tyme (seeing the tyme alloted for it was spent in treating wth ye Comissary), not out of any disrespect to ye service, wch he himselfe did usually attend at other tymes.

When the wolfe complained that the Lamb had fouled the water that he was to drinke, the Lambe answered that if he had defiled it, yet that could not prejudice the wolfe that was above it, for the mud would certeynly descend downwards : But this answer did not fill the hungry belly of the wolfe.

M^r.

M^r. Preston's innocency did agravate his crime, wch was his popularity; and, therefore, they told him they were bound to support by all just meanes the Bishop's jurisdiction; that the King had honoured him in leaving that affront to be examined by his prop̅p̅ judges, and that except he could take off the Court, they must and would proceed to a very round and serious censure! That a fellow of a College for preaching of an innocent and honest sermon, in a church belonging to the College, by the consent & in the hearing of the Incumbent, should be thus vigourously prosecuted, was something hard.

Among many other gentlemen of quality that were Pupils unto M^r. Preston at this tyme, there was one Sr Capel Bedels, an orphan, of a very faire estate in Huntingtonshire, a daughter's son of old Sr Arthur Capel; who, being Guardian

Doctr Preston. 49

Guardian to his grandchild, had recom-
ended him, as he had done many of
his owne sons, unto his goverment; it
was a great trust, & M^r. Preston's care
was answerable; and, because "plus vi-
dent oculi," he had his spyes, that gave
him notice of all their carriages &
correspondencies; by one of these he
was informed that Sir Capell haunted
D^r. Newcomb's howse, and was familliar
wth his daughter, M^{rs}. Jane Newcomb,
a very propp well bred gentlewoman;
his Tutor asked if they were contracted,
he answered "no, but would be very
shortly, for he was resolved to have
her."

M^r. Preston charges him to keepe all
secret, that Sr Capel might not think he
was acquainted wth it; and imediatly
appoints a journey unto Saffron Wal-
den, to take the ayre and see that
stately building at Audley End, & tooke
divers of his fellow comoners alonge,
as

as he had done at other tymes, and
amonge others this Sr Capel Bedles ;
When they had dined & viewed the
Howse, it was propounded by one of
them that they might goe that night
to Haddam & visit old Sr Arthur Capel,
seeing they were thus farr on their way
& it was late ; M^r. Preston seemed to
be indifferent, and so the proposition
tooke ; and wth none more than S^r
Capel, who knew his grandfather would
fill his pockets, and that would sweeten
his Newcomb mistress' Embraces, and
make him welcomb to her.

The old knight was glad to Enterteyne such welcom guests, & that night
there was no discourse but of the stately
roomes, & goodly gallery at Audley
End, & so the young gentleman went
to bedd pleased that the college bell
would not waken him ; but M^r. Preston slept not, "in utrumque aurem,"
but awakened betimes, & acquaints S^r
Arthur

Arthur wth all the business, adviseth w^th
him by no meanes to p̅mit the gentleman's retorn͜e to ye college, for though
ye wound might seeme quite cured, &
he never so much engage forbearance,
yet frequent apparitions would redinte-
grate. "Et nihil facilius quam amor
recrudescit."

Sir Arthur was a very wise man, &
had experience of ye world, thanks M^r.
Preston for his faithfulness, pretends S^r
Capel wanted some thinge, and desires
his tutor to give him leave to stay a
little tyme untill he could be furnished,
& then he should be sent; to which M^r.
Preston easily consented, & so the rest
retorned; after which the old Knight
told Sr Capel that he began to grow
a man, and it would be fit for him to
travayle before he setled, & so pre-
vailes wth him to be content. But what
saith M^rs. Newcomb who is rob'd by this
means of her vowed and resolved servant,

vant, & her crafty father that beholds
so good a morsell snacht from betweene
his teeth ? Doe you thinke he had forgotten this when M^r. Preston came to
preach wthin his jurisdiction ? Other
injuryes phaps may be forgotten, but
loss of mony is not. " Ploratur lachry-
mis amissa pecunia veris."

M^r. Preston was no stranger altogether at Court ; However now there
was no remedy. When he came to Newmarket, he found that Bishop Andrews,
then Bishop of Ely, was Cheife ; & his
jurisdiction, in the Commissary, was it
that was pretended to be affronted ; and
therefore applyed himself to him, &
told him that he did not purpose to
offend, but being engaged for to preach
at that tyme, could not wth honour dis-
appoint the Auditory ; if he suspected
him, for anythinge, he desired he would
examine him, & satisfy himselfe. The
Bishop told him that ye King was informed

formed he was an enimy to formes of Prayer, & held no prayer lawfull but what was conceived, &, therefore, being popular, his judgement & opinion might doe hurt.

Mr. Preston answered that it was a slaunder, for he thought set formes lawfull, and refused not to be present at ye college prayer; The Bishop answered that he was glad, & would informe the King, and doe him all ye good he could, & bade him wayte awhile, and then repaire to him againe for satisfaction in it; and so tyme passed on, & there was nothing done. There were some at Court that wisshed well to Mr. Preston, as Dr. Young, an honest Scotchman, that was Deane of Winchester; who told Mr. Preston plainly that Bpp Andrews was his greatest Adversary, and, though he gave him good wordes, yet he assured the King that if Mr. Preston were not for this expelled ye University, Lord Bps

Bishop Andrews his double-dealing with Mr. Preston.

Bp[s] would not long continue. But M[r]. Preston was accounted (& not w[th]out cause) a learned man, and therefore the Bishop was not willing to appeare against him; yet desired the punishment might be inflicted where the fact was done, and that in y[e] University.

Mr. Preston's resolute application to the Bishop.

Master Preston saw now that y[e] Bishop was a courtier, & could afforde wordes where deeds were not intended, & therefore goes again to the Bishop, & tells him plainly that he or none must put a period to his attendance; and that either he would speake to the King in his behalfe, or tell him plainly that he would not, that he might know from whence all his trouble flowed. The Bishop paused awhile on this bold carriadge, and at last bade him come to him at such a tyme againe, & he would deale with y[e] King in his behalfe. So he goes to the King, & tells him, that

that however Mr. Preston was very dangerous & it would be a very great security if he were handsomly expelled,
yet he doubted it would not beare well
should it be done for this offence ; for
he would be absolved in the mynds &
opinions of men, & be owned and applauded as their martyr, & might phaps
recover & live to be revenged ; & therefore thought it would be better for to
enjoyne him to declare his judgemᵗ as
to formes of prayer, for that would be
accounted a Recantation, & would
weaken his Reputation wᵗʰ yᵉ Puritans ; wᶜʰ would be enough ; for, if
they could divide him from his party,
they should not feare him ; for he said
his carriadge argued confidence in some
assistance, wᶜʰ when they had removed,
they should be strong enough at single
hand.

All that yᵉ Bpp spake was as if " ex
tripode ;" an order, therefore, was presently

sently drawne & sent to yᵉ Vice Chancelor, that Mʳ. Preston should in Buttolph's church declare his judgement about Formes of Prayer, on such a Sunday, or else they should imediately proceede against him according to their first instructions.

Mʳ. Preston was glad there was a way out, yet sensible of yᵉ hard hand that had bin carryed towards him ; but now there was no remedy ; & in vaine was it to strive against yᵉ streame. Before he could get home, the newes was all about yᵉ towne that Mʳ. Preston was to preach a recantation sermon at Buttolph's church on such a day. This was good sporte to yᵉ brave blades, who now came crowding as fast as any for to heare, and no sin now for any to be absent from prayer ; and indeed there was a very great assembly, though he did all he could to have concealed it. He went on upon his former text

&

& preached a very profitable sermon concerning growing in Grace, & directed prayer as a speciall means to it. And this, he said, was of two sortes; Either that wch was suddaine, extempory, and conceived; or, set, enjoyned, & prescribed before, not only for the sense & scope, but also words and phrases; And, whereas some thought this was to stint ye Spirit, he said there was a liberty to use conceived prayer at other times, wherein the spirit might expatiate & enlarge itself, though not in extension & variety of language.

The p͞sons who came to laugh had little cause to doe it; for this passage was at ye very close of the sermon; all before being both sharpe & searching. Both sides went home sylent, & not without some prynts of good upon many of their spirits. "Optimus orator censandus, non qui meruit auditorem judicium, sed qui abstulit." He makes

y^e

yᵉ best speech that binds his hearers rather to thinke what was said than who said it.

The good fellows were nothing so merry at the end, as at yᵉ beginning of yᵒ sermon. Indifferent hearers praised all, & were confirmed in a good opinion of the Preacher; good men were glad he came off so well, and was at liberty to preach again where they might heare him; Himselfe was troubled lest any thinge he had said should be mistaken or misinterpreted, as he was apt to be; But there were many eyes upon this action, and all wayted to see the issue. The Courtiers did not like it that, after such tossings too & fro, he should thus light upon his feete; yet would not meddle for yᵉ present, but wayt occasions; those who were well affected, were glad he was engaged against the Court and Bishops, & did presage he might be instrumentall to their downfall;

fall ; every one laboured to engage him more & more against them.

The Spanish match was then yᵉ Comōn talke, & great averseness appeared in yᵉ generality of people. Dʳ. Willet had presumed to offer arguments to the King against matching wᵗʰ Idolaters; the King was greatly vexed at this adventure, & tooke great pains to convince the Docter that a Papist was no Idolater : "sed non persuadebat etiam si persuaserat." The people were dissatisfied, &, there being then a Parliament, a very honᵇˡᵉ and able member of yᵉ howse of Lords prevayled wᵗʰ Mʳ. Preston to write some arguments against it ; and, though there were very severe edicts & Proclamations against scandelous papers, & intermedling wᵗʰ matters of state, yet he promised it should be scattered & divulged unto fit p̄sons, and none should know from whence or whom it came. Accordingly,

Accordingly, when it was finished, & written faire, one gave it to a porter whom he met in Holborne, & bad him leave it according to ye direction. The next day a great Lord came unto him that had p͞swaded M^r. Preston unto the service, and tells him that he had met wth such a peece against ye Spanish match as he never saw, & protested that he was convinced, & would speake against it in ye Howse, whatever came of it. The other asked him who made it, & where he had it, he assured him he knew not, but it was left at his lodging by he knew not whom; the Lord desired he might see it, & so it was coppyed out & spreade among those of ye Parliament they thought fit, but the Authour of it never knowne.

King James had something always in his speeches and writings against the Puritans, wch was ill taken, for that it was apparent that those meant thereby

thereby were godly and conscientious p̄sons.

The howse of Comons was the only mote in King James his eye, the "Re-mora" (as he conceived) unto his abso-lute dominion ; for he knew not how to engage them as he had done ye Law-yers and Divines ; but if he stopt one mouth wth preferment this Parliament, there would be others open ye next against him. There were some now that adventured to apologize for Puritans, & to say in Parliament that honest men were wounded under that name, & to propose that Godly ministers might not be silenced & throwne out of their freeholds for tryfles & ceremonyes. But King James would have none of that stuffe, and therefore breaks up the Parliam^t, & sets out proclamations. But people love not to be forced to duty, "Homines duci volunt non cogi."

The

The King's designe to make the schollars his, as he had done ye lawyers, in order to the making himselfe absolute.

The Chaplines that attended monthly at Court, were not ambitious of preaching very often ; and so a combination was agreed on for Preachers before the King, whenever he should lye wthin 12 miles of Cambridge. The King did not despaire of making Scholars his, and therefore used all endeavours to obleidge them, especially Cambridge men, where a seed of Puritans had been a long time; and though ye plaines about Newmarket afforded better winter game than elsewhere, yet schollars, he conceived, might be catcht sometimes as well as hares; and so willing they should preach before him. Young men he knew would preach themselves, "omnis oratio docet, aut rem, aut animum dicentis;" and thus he should learne either thinges or p̄sons.

By this means it came to M^r. Preston's turn to preach before the King at Royston, he was so mufled at Court

in

in D^r. Newcomb's business, that he knew
not what to doe ; he could not declyne
it altogether, for that would have exposed him unto too much observation,
and yet he greatly feared what might
befall him in ye doing of it ; therefore
he changed his course with one that
was to preach a little after, & did it
very privately, that if his enemys should
have designes, they might be disappointed ; and so it was not much knowne
when he was to preach.

It fell out that his course came upon a
Tewsday, when the King was at Hintch-
ingbrook ; the Court was very thin, the
Prince & Duke of Buckingham both
abroad, and the King himselfe was for
a hunting match that day, and gave
order that the sermon should begin at
eight aclock. Master Preston had some
at court that were solicitous as well as
he, & they told him it would give very
great content if he would take some
occasion

occasion in the sermon to shew his judgement, as he had done before, about set formes. D^r. Young, Deane of Winchester (of whom I spake before) did then attend, and when the King came in & sate down in the chaire, he told him who it was that preached, & said he hoped he would give content. I pray God he doth, said the King. His text was Jo^n 1. 16. "And of his fulness have all we received, and grace for grace;" wch he so cleerely opened, & applyed, that the King sate all ye while very quiet, & never stirred or spake to anybody, but by his lookes discovered he was pleased.

When all was done, he came unto him as the manner was to kisse his hand, when ye King asked him of what Preston he was descended? he answered of that in Lancashire; then said the King, you have many of yor name and kindred very eminent, and Preston the
Priest

Priest, although a Papist, is a very learned man.

Great hast was made to bring in dynner, and the King was very pleasant all the tyme, had his eye continually on Mr. Preston, & spake of divers pas-sadges in the sermon wth much content; specially that of the Arminians putting God into the same extremity that Darius was put in (Dan. 6.) when he would have saved Daniel but could not. But, as soone as ever Mr. Preston was retyred, the Marquess Hamilton kneeled downe, and besought the King that he might comend the Preacher to him for his Chaplyn; protested that he did not know him, but that he was moved by the weight & strength of that he had delivered; told him that he spake no pen & Inckorne language, but as one that comprehended what he said, and that he could not but have substance & matter in him. The King acknowledged

ledged all, but said it was too early, remembered Newmarket busyness, & was reserved.

Sir Ralf Freeman, one of ye Mas^trs of Requests, had marryed a kinswoman of ye Duke of Buckingham's, & was a kinsman unto M^r. Preston; he makes relation of y^o business unto the Duke, & told him if now he would appeare in favour of his cousin Preston, he might obleidge the Puritans, & lay a groundworke to his owne security, if tempests should arise; assured him that M^r. Preston was ingenuous, & that ye King & all ye court were taken wth the sermon, and did approve it. The Duke of Buckingham was a wise man, apprehensive of what Sr Ralf suggested seasonably, saw those they called Puritans were growing, and in the Parliament were thought considerable; knew that ye King's affection might coole, & he neede friends; he therefore tooke

S^r

Sʳ Ralf's discourse into his most serious thoughts. An honest man one Mʳ. Packer was then his secretary, & he set on what Sʳ Ralf Freeman had suggested ; and so it came unto a resolution that Mʳ. Preston should be owned. The Duke comanded Sʳ Ralf Freeman to goe to Mʳ. Preston from him, and acquaint him wᵗʰ his good opinion of him, and that he desired to see him. Indeed there was such a concurrence & concentring of oppinions & desires amonge the courtiers, that it was assured Mʳ. Preston that he might be Chaplin unto whom he would ; and it was now only a deliberation which of these offers he should accept, and whom he would acknowledge his Patron & Protector for the tyme to come.

There was not so few clergymen at any tyme at Court, and so no kind of opposition ; yet the King himselfe hung back, & would doe nothing hastily ; he

was

was not reconcilable to the Puritans, and so desired not in that respect for to engage him. Yet he desired to deprive the Puritans of M^r. Preston, & so divide him from them; and would doe any thinge that might drive on that. Besides considering how many M^r. Preston had wonne, that he was a young man & might be drawne on, he would not therefore hinder or oppose his advancement. So it was the joynt oppinion that the best preferment was to be the Prince's chaplin, who then was growne & had a howsehold.

This therefore was represented unto Sr Ralf Freeman and his oppinion required; who quickly yeelded & proposed it to ye Duke. Both Prince & Duke had bin abroad, & neither of them had heard of ye sermon. When therefore M^r. Preston was brought unto ye Duke, he very seriously received him;

him ; told him it was the Prince's un-
happiness & his to be absent when
he did preach ; & therefore desired him
that he would voutsafe a coppy of his
sermon to him ; and beleeve that he
would be ready to the best and utmost
of his power to serve him.

There were many other courtiers that
desired coppyes of ye sermon ; and, y^e
court not staying there, Master Preston
came home to furnish coppies. He never
penned sermon word for word, but
wrote what came into his mynde, and
as it came, & that in no good hand, &
so it was a business to provide these
coppies ; wch yet, he seriously attended
untill they were written faire, and then
goes to court, where the Duke presents
him to ye Prince ; and so he was made
& admitted chaplin to ye Prince in ordinary, for as then the Prince had not
compleated the number he intended,
wch was six ; these were each intended
to

to wayt two months by the yeare, to preach unto yᵉ howsehold upon yᵉ Lord's days, & p̄forme such dutyes as were required of them.

But God was making other worke for Mʳ. Preston; for Doctor Tolson, Bishop of Salisbury, dyes, and leaves a wife and many children unprovided for, for he had bin Bishop but a little while. This wife of his was Dʳ. Davenant's sister; in pitty, therefore, & comisseration of her ̄case, it was proposed to the King, by those that were his friends, that Doctor Davenant, a single man & well deserving, might succeed his brother in the Bishoprick; and so make some provision for his children. The King thought very well of Doctor Davenant, not only for his singular abillities & labours in the University, but for his paines also & service in the Synod of Dort against Arminius: and it was looked on as a deed of charity, & so beleeved

beleeved he would carry it. But this created Mr. Preston cares ; Dr. Davenant had bin his constant & faithfull friend, & given countenance upon all occasions to him & all his pupils ; but now who should succeed, & where should Mr. Preston find another shelter. The fellows for the most p̄te were not his friends, envyed his numbers, & great relations, & there was no man like so to befriend him. The Margaret professor's place would be voyd also by this remove, and many able stirring batchelrs in divinity proposed unto Mr. Preston that place, and assured him that the election would be easily carryed for him.

The truth is, he had no great hope to doe any great good in the election of the Master of the College ; & one Dr. Mansel being named, a very moderate goodnatured man, he let that care fall, & was more anxious about the professor's place ; for though sound doctrine

doctrine in the University was of much use, yet English preaching was like to worke more, and win more soules to God.

He always highly vallued and frequently consulted wth M^r. Dod, who p̄swaded him that English preaching was that wherein God was more immediately served ; he said there were others that might supply the University in the Professor's place, that either could not, or would not labour for men's conversion. The Master of Sidney College, D^r. Ward, a vast schollar, was then in vieu & nomination for the Professor's place. Yet M^r. Preston was so solicited by honest men to hold it that he knew not what to doe. Two thinges he thought he wanted to enable him, the one was a Latine tongue, the other a Latine stile ; in both w^ch, by reason of desuetude, he was unready in. For his style, therefore, he resolves upon

an

an exact & logical analysis of all the
epistles, wch would actuate and exercise
his style, & acquaint him wth the Scripture phrase & language, and which, if he
were called to be professor, might serve
for lectures in the schooles. This worke
he imediately applyed himselfe unto,
and very happily compleated ; a great
worke of paines unto him, & in itselfe of
great worth ; but being Latin & written
only wth his owne ill hand, was not
thought popular enough to come abroad,
and so lyeth in the darke.

For the exercise of his Latin tongue
he resolves a journey into the Netherlands, where he should have much occasion of speaking Latin, & so see
those Colleges and universityes. But
there was no traveyling beyond sea
without a license under ye hands of
Privy Counsellors ; this he procures
amonge his friends wth all ye secrecy
that could be, and a great while before
he

he meant to use it, that he might conceale it from ye college & University. But this his secrecy begat suspition that there was some plot, and it was resented so much ye more because no clergyman was made acquainted wth it. The opinion was, that something was brewing against Episcopacy. This they were sure of, that Amsterdam was in the Netherlands, and ever had bin fatall to the Hierarchy.

The Lord keeper then was Bishop Williams, he sees this plague afarr of. Prov. 22. 3. and provides a messenger to goe alonge, unknowne to M^r. Preston, that should observe & give intelligence weekly of all that passed. " Integer vitæ scelerisque purus, non eget jaculis nec arcu." "A breastplate of righteousness is a better guard than a shirt or coate of mayle." It was David's uprightness that did preserve him. Psal. 25. 21. So was it M^r. Preston's, for he

he knew nothing of this attendance untill after his retorne. He gave out in
the college, & amonge his pupils, that
he would goe the next vacation into
Kent to visit Sr Richard Sands, &
drinke, if he saw cause, of ye Turne-
bridge Waters. He concludes also to
take one of his pupils wth him, a York-
shire gentleman, Sr Henry Slingsby his
son and heyre, & did accordingly acquaint his father, & make provision
for it long before.

The tyme came, & he goes into Kent,
& is received in ye passadge boat for
Roterdam, in the garb & notion of a
gentleman, wth his scarlet cloake, gold
hat band, & all thinges answerable ; &
so goes over all the Provinces both Protestant & Popish, where there was anythinge observable, & encounters frequently wth divers Priests & Jesuits,
professing himselfe a Protestant gentleman that was willing to finde out the
truth

truth & try all Tenents; and accordingly was courted by them very much,
and solicited to be a Papist, to w^ch
end they gave him very many Popish
bookes; and so he came backe to Kent,
& to ye college at the time appointed;
unknowne to any of ye College, but
only to one of his pupils from whom
he seldom concealed anythinge. He
was no sooner setled in ye college, but
a rumour flyes abroad that M^r. Preston
had bin beyond the seas; he shewed
them that it was incredible, & woundred
at their sillyness, that they would beleeve so unlikely a relation. The matter was not great now all was past, &
so it rested doubtfull & undetermined.

He had a long tyme beene successfull
in pupils, but D^r. Davenant's leaving
of ye college troubled him. A great
tutor hath much occasion to use the
Master's influence, for accomodation &
advancement of his pupils, wch now
he

he saw he could not promise unto him-selfe. And it fell out much about this tyme, that Doctor Dun, Preacher of Lincoln's Inn, dyed; when some in that society proposed y^t M^r. Preston might be tryed whether he were willing to accept of that place for Tearme tyme. He was himselfe neither carelcss nor cracking of his good name, " Famæ nec incuriosus nec venditator," but it was much growne by reason of his success in the conflicts & encounters he had at court.

It was some refreshing unto honest men, that M^r. Preston, so resolute & constante in ye ways of God, was yet the Prince's Chaplaine; and it suited wth him to have an oppṫumity to exer-cise his ministry in a considerable & intelligent congregation; were he was assured many Parlam^t men, & others of his best acquaintance would be his hearers; & where, in Tearme time, he should

Mr. Preston desir-ed to be Lecturer to the Lawyers at Lin-coln's Inn.

should be well accomodated ; so he consented & undertooke the place. The chapple then was very little, and at first the numbers that attended on his minestry, besides their owne society, were few ; but when the chapple was new built, as now it is, the numbers were exceeding great that were his constant hearers, & foundations layd that will not easily be ruyned.

This was some ease to his grieved mynde, for D^r. Davenant's leaving of ye college & University ; but fitted not his great capacity & lardge desire of doing good. The College he gave over in his thoughts, but not the University, where his preaching was much resented and made great impressions; and though at Lincoln's Inn he had gownmen to be his hearers, yet they were not like to propogate & spread it. A preacher in the University doth generate "Patres," begets begetters, & transmits unto posterity

terity what God is pleased to reveale to him. In a word, doth what the Apostle doth enjoyne, 2 Tim. 2. 2. Thus Mr. Preston thirsted after oppertunityes of doing service ; and might say with the Spouse, that he was sick of love, Cant. 2. 5.

Some of the fellows of Emanuel College were very eminent for p̄ts & learning, & yet clowded & obscured (as they thought) by an oppinion that lay upon the college, that they were Puritans ; that is, not only godly and religious, for so they were, & were content to be esteemed, but Non-conformists, and averss to government ; for wch cause there had bin lately some alteration made, both in their chapple and manner of diet. They thought, therefore, that, if they could prevaile wth Dr. Chaderton their present master to resigne (who was established in it by ye founder, and named in ye statute,

but

but growne very old, & had outlived many of those great relations wch he had before), they might p̄haps procure that M^r. Preston might succeede him, & bring ye college into reputation. For M^r. Preston was a good man (though a courtier), the Prince his chapline, & very gratious with ye Duke of Buckingham. But this was sooner said than done.

The old Doctor was exceeding wary & jealous, not only of his owne disparagement, but especially of the good & welfare of that brave foundation, that had growne & flourished under his government so long. For, if it were but knowne that he were out, there were divers lay in wayt to get a mandate & come in against the mynds of the fellows. A fresh example whereof they had lately seen in their next neighbo^r Christ's college, where, after M^r. Pemberton was chosen, D^r. Carew, Deane of

of Exeter, was imposed on them, &
did all he could to mould anew and
alter the constitution and genius of the
college. Therefore, one of yᵉ fellows
answred that this might be better hin-
dred & prevented while he was alive
then at his deate; for his resignation
might be carryed privately, but his
death could not; and, if all yᵉ fellows
were agreed, the election might be past
before the resignation was discovered;
& so they promissed to sound & try
the judgement of the other fellows, and
then repaire againe to him.

There were two things in yᵉ college
that (in their opinions) greatly pintched
them, the one was the statute of attendance & continuance while they were
fellows, so that they had not opptuni-
tyes to live in noblemen's howses, or
take lectures to exercise their ministry,
& make themselves knowne unto such
as had it in their power to prefer them.

Another

Another was the statute of departing at such a standing, whether they were provided or no; and there was then a fresh example in Docto^r Traverse, a man of great worth, yet forced to sojourne as a fellow comoner in Christ's College untill he could be better accomodated. The fellows therefore were easily induced to affect this change, for they thought that M^r. Preston might be an instrument, by reason of his great acquaintance, either to get some mitigation of the statute, or procure more livings to be annexed to the college for their preferment.

So they retorned to the old man, and told him that ye fellows were all agreed, and ready to doe what he should prescribe, and that it rested now in him to prevent ye danger that did threaten, not only them in their p̄ticcular concernements, but the growing good & welfare also of ye college. The poore old

old man knew not what to doe; to
outlive the mastership he thought was
to outlive himselfe, & to goe into
his grave alive; yet he honoured &
loved M^r. Preston very much, and could
not answer that dilemma of ye college
safely; therefore, he told them he would
not be wanting to ye College good; but
it concerned them as well as himselfe
to provide that they were not cheated,
& another forced on them, whether they
would or not; and, therefore, desired
that M^r. Preston might be requested to
deale wth his friends at Court, & procure
some promise y^t there should be no
mandate granted in case his resignation
should be knowne.

He told them likewise how unprovided he was for maintenance when
that was gone, & how unseemly it
would be for him now in his old age
to want, and, therefore, in this p̄ticcular
desired he might be taken into consideration.

sideration. But M^r. Preston quickly eased the old man of all these feares, by procuring a L^{re} to him from the Duke of Buckingham in these wordes.

"S^r,

"I have moved his Matie concerning Master Preston's succeeding of you in the mastership of Emanuel college; who is not only willing, but also gratiously pleased to recomend him to ye place in especiall manner before any other; so that in making this way for him, you shall doe a very acceptable thinge to his Matie: as also to the Prince, his master, of wch I am likewise to give notice; and, to put you out of all doubt that another may be imposed on you, you shall not neede to feare any thinge in reguard that from his Matie there will be no hindrance to his succession.

"And for that point of supply of maintenance, I shall (as I promised) take
care

care for to procure it, when fit occasion
shall be offered ; so, taking kindly what
you have done, I rest

         " GEORGE BUCKINGHAM.

   " *Theobalds, Sep.* 20. 1662."

When the Doct^r had received & read
this letter, he was in all thinges satisfied as to the Court; but they all knew
that D^r. Traverse lay in wayt for this
preferment; for, being outed by the statute of Emanuel college, he soujourned
as a fellow Comoner at Christ's College,
& presumed, either by his friends at
Court to get a mandate, or be chosen in
ye college by a p͞ty of ye fellows whom he
thought his owne ; therefore great care
was taken to keepe all secret; and
though ye Statute doe ordaine a vacancy
of seaven days, & notice by a schedule
passed upon the Chapple doore; yet,
such was the concurrent uniforme agree-
ment of all the fellows, that it was not
discovered to any of the schollars,
                        untill

untill the day of election ; &, because there is a sacrament to be imediately before it, they were constreyned to lock upp all the gates, that none might come in nor out till it was past; and then two of ye fellows were dispatched to Queen's College, to acquaint M^r. Preston wth what they had done, & to desire that at two of ye clock he would repaire to ye college to be admitted, & undertake the charge.

The Doct^r chosen M^r of Emanuel College in Cambridge.

It was strange newes at Queen's, and all ye college were much affected wth it, woundring extreamely that so great a transaction should be carryed wth so much secrecy, & that amonge M^r. Preston's twelve disciples (as they called them) there should be never a Judas, but all concenter in it. But there was order given presently that all ye schollars should be ready against two of ye clock that day to attend M^r. Preston & the fellows to Emanuel College,

lege, in habits sutable to their severall qualityes; wch was done accordingly, and a very great company attended him from Queen's to Emanuel, where they were cheerfully received & enterteyned according to the custome, wth a generous and costly banquet; and then retorned to Queen's againe, but left M^{r}. Preston, the prop & glory of it, at Emanuel.

In the plantation of Emanuel College at the first, the godly founder tooke great care to store his Colledge wth Godly and able fellows from all other colleges, & some were after added that were eminent; but, now a master is bestowed; God in mercy hath enabled that good society to pay their debts, by sending not only members, but also heads into very many of the other colleges; so as they may well now say, "Quæ Regio in terris nostri non plena Laboris."

S^{r}

S͏ͬ Walter Mildemay, their noble &
religious founder, was wont to say unto
his friends that he had set an acorne
that might p̄haps in tyme become an
oake. And, blessed be God, our eyes
have scene it not only growne &
flourishing, but fruitfull; seasonable
showers (a great promotion unto a new
plantation), and earnest prayers unto
God (a speciall meanes to bring these
downe), have in these last yeares retorned unto this college a glorious har-
vest. To God be praise !

This newes ran swiftly all yᵉ kingdom
over, & was received as men were affected; good men were glad yᵗ honest
men were not abhorred as they had
bin at yᵉ court, & presaged much of
that enlardgement & deliverance we
have lived to see. Yᵉ Courtiers made
full account that he was theirs, &
would mount up from one step to another untill he were a Prelate; especially
the

the Duke of Buckingham, who, from
this tyme, seemed much to affect him,
thinking he had given earnest, and
could not be defrauded of his purchase
of him. The Earl of Pembrook & Countess of Bedford also had a great interest
in him, & he in them. In short all
men looked on him as a rising man, &
respected him accordingly.

As for Lincoln's Inn, they made account they had a speciall influence
into this honour, as having first ex-
pressed their good opinion of him;
and there was an honest godly old
man, Master Ayres, one of the Benchers
there, that, upon hearing of the newes,
would needes be young againe, and
make an anagram on his name, though
he was uncerteine how he writ it in
Latin, for he had seene it written divers
wayes; being, therefore, resolute, &
loath to miss it, he resolves to write it
both wayes; as he that used to say his
prayers

prayers in Latin & English, that both might not faile ; and so first he writ it, " Johannes Prestonius," with this ana-gram *,—

" En stas pius in honore,"and this distich,
" Doctrina ingenium virtus tuæ præmia
      poscunt,
En dedit Emanuel, stas in honore pius."

But, lest he should be mistaken, he writes Johannes Prestonus with this anagram,—

" Se nosse non turpia," and this distich,
" Turpia non novisse, bonum, se nosce
      beatum,
Ista doces alios, sed prius ipse facis."

The rest of the society rejoyced that their lecturer was Master of Emanuel ; & tooke occasion to express it, accord-ing to their severall relations & dispo-sitions, when he came to them in the Terme wch shortly followed.

---

* Transcribed literally from the manuscript.

There

There was one thinge in the college statutes wch greatly troubled him, and that was, that the master's absence from the college was confined to a month in every quarter; and he saw not how he could attend at court, & preach at Lincolne's Inn in Tearme time, but he should transgress; but the fellows soone agreed to an interpretation that absolved him from the rigid sense; there being in the statute a double liberty; first, that in case of violent detention it should not hold; they resolved that not only a naturall, but also a morall violence was to be understood; the other was, that in case of College business he should not be esteemed absent.

Now the 'college at that tyme was in suite for a living in the West, of good vallue, wth one M^r. Ewins, a gentleman in the parrish, who had bred up a younger son to be a schollar in relation to that living; & therefore contended

tended for it, as if it had beene his owne inheritance; and, when he was worsted at Comon Law, prefers a Bill in Chancery, & thought by mony to carry it against the College right. Bishop Williams, Lord Keeper then, was his great friend, and when, after many delayes, it came to hearing, he would not allow the Councel for ye College to speake. M^r. Preston, being present, craved leave to speake in the cause himselfe, but was not only sylenced, but severely reprehended for it.

It was Trinity Terme, & the Plague very hot in London, so that Michelmas Terme was wholy adjourned, and the next Terme was proclaymed at Redding, & ye Records removed thither; but, before that, the Lord Keeper was removed from his throne, and Sr Thomas Coventry, one of ye college Councell that were not p̄mitted before to speake, succeeded him; by whose integrity

integrity & justice the College were restored to their right, wᶜʰ ever since they enjoyed ; and so Mʳ. Preston's following of the College business excused his absence all this time.

Being, therefore, now established, and greatly mynding yᵉ good thereof, he observed that the schollars had kept Acts but seldome, and accordingly when they came unto it, p̄formed it but meanly; he, therefore, advised wᵗʰ the Fellows in it, and, after many consultations, it was resolved that the number of Acts should be in a manner doubled, of those under Masters of Art ; wᶜʰ was a great advancemᵗ to learning of all sortes in the college. About this tyme Sʳ Arthur Chichester, afterwards an Irish Baron, was chosen to goe Embassador into Germany about the Palatinate Affaires, & Mʳ. Preston was by the Duke of Buckingham and other friends designed to goe along with him ; he did not greatly

greatly fancy the employment, yet would not contradict it. Only it was considered that though he was the Prince's Chaplin & master of a college, yet he was not Doctor, wch they thought might sound ill abroad, and reflect upon his Master. There was not tyme enough to goe unto this business in the ordinary way of Acts & exercises, therefore a mandate was sent to the Vice Chancellor & Heads, that, for as much as M^r. Preston was to wayte upon the Lord Embassador, & could not in so short a tyme p̄forme his Acts, he should be forthwth admitted D^r in Divinity, that he might be ready to attend the service; wch was done accordingly wth all alacrity.

Being, therefore, thus engaged, & not knowing what might befall him in ye voyadge, he resolved to settle his temporall estate before he went; he was not willing to be accounted rich, & would often say, "Manifestus thesaurus cito

cito expenditur;" &, therefore, though he had great incombs from his pupils, & was not prodigal, yet he was not master of his mony; for he had bin advised to adventure in the East India Company, then newly set up, &, because that estates there were the more invisible, he was the willinger; but by that means wanted mony, for there was paying for many yeares, but no retornes; yet there was hope it might at last come in, and so it did without diminution of the principle, yet not in his life tyme. He therefore thought it needful to make a legal disposition of his estate by will, and so he did, and named a very honourable p̄son his executor, who lived to enjoy that mony, as well other, by virtue thereof.

But the voyadge came to nothing, for Sr Arthur did not goe as he intended; yet this was Doctr Preston's last will, & according to it all was enjoyed;

joyed; though he made additions by way of request or direction, wch were accordingly p̄formed.

It was ever Doct^r Preston's ambition not to be mercenary in his ministry, but at liberty to preach where he might doe most good, without relation or respect to wages; and he considered that the master of Emanuel could have no living that had cure of soules annexed. He, therefore, was willing to give eare unto ye sollicitations of ye townesmen, who greatly pressed him to be their Lecturer at Trinity church.

They had applied themselves formerly to D^r. Andrews, Bishop of Ely, and propounded unto him M^r. Jefferyes as lecturer, one of ye fellows of Pembroke Hall; who gave admittance, and Mast^r Jefferyes preached there for some yeares; M^r. Jefferyes, however, was desirous of a more settled condition, and desired

desired D^r. Preston to procure him to
be chaplin to some noble man, that was
like to helpe him to a living; wch was
a very easy thinge for the Docter to
doe ; who, accordingly, presented him
to Marquess Hamilton, and accepted
him with much respect, as well for D^r.
Preston's sake as his owne. Nor was
it long before a living fell, wch was the
Rectory of Dunmow in Essex ,wch the
Marquess procured, & bestowed upon
his chaplin, M^r. Jeffereys ; and by that
means the Lecture at Trinity was shortly
to be voyd.

The townsmen at Cambridge made
accorunt they now had what they desired, namely an opptunity to settle
D^r. Preston in the Lecture at Trinity;
& great care was taken to encrease
the stypend from fifty pounds a yeare
to fower score, that the D^r. might have
£20 a quarter paid to him, as thinking
the former inconsiderable, & not knowing

ing what principles the D^r. lived by;
and when they had effected that, they
imployed some of the chiefe to propose
the matter to the D^r. very sollemnely;
who was easily p̄swaded to accept their
offer, w^thout relation to the stipend.
But there was one of ye fellows of
Sidney College, Master Middlethwaite,
that put in for it; and, though none of
the contributors or townsmen sided w^th
him, yet he procured letters from the
Bishop of Ely, & engaged all his friends
both in ye Court and University; so
that it came unto a very great contest.

D^r. Preston, who was offered any Bishoprick he would resolve on, & told
at Royston by the Duke of Buckingham
that ye Bishoprick of Glocester was then
voyd, contends wth M^r. Middlethwaite
to be Lecturer of Trinity church, for a
stypend of fower score pounds a yeare,
as the upshot of all his hopes, & fruit
of all his great atchievements at Court.
The

The contention was so great on all sides that it could not be concluded by any mediation, but was referred to a hearing at Royston, before King James, who was really against the Dr.'s preaching in the University ; the consequence whereof Doct^r Preston well saw, & was informed fully of. I confess I often wondered why M^r. Middlethwaite, an eminent schollar, and like enough to get preferment, as afterwards it's knowne he did, should stickle for so small an oppertunity to preach, against the inclination & disposition of ye townsmen ; untill I understood that he was set on by y^o Prelaticall Heads, who told him that it was a service acceptable to the King, & he should be rewarded for it. At the tyme appointed it came unto a hearing, and an argument urged against the Docter that it was a lecture mainteyned by six-pences, a thinge unseemely for a master of a college, & the Prince's Chaplin.

But

But the Duke had taken care that nothing should be ordered & concluded against yᵉ Dr.'s minde; for the Duke resolved not to loose him. So the meeting was dissolved, and nothing done.

But that night Sʳ Edward Conoway, then Secretary, invited Dʳ. Preston to supp, and after supper, told him that the King had ordered him to tell him that if he would give over his p̄suance of that lecture, & let the Heads dispose of it, he should make his choyce of any other preferment that was more honourable and profitable for him. But the Dr.'s end was to doe good, not to get goods; the King's to make him useless & divide him from the Puritans. The Duke was more indifferent, who laboured in him to win & gratify the Puritans, whose power in Parliament was now growne very formidable. Therefore, when nothing else would content him, he was confirmed Lecturer at Trinity

nity church ; the last preferment he ever had ; where he preached afterwards all his tyme, & did much good.

The Duke had now obleiged Dr. Preston, in the judgemt & opinion of all the honest p̄ty, & much displeased the Prelaticall ; & he saw, apparently, that King James approved not his siding wth him ; yet was he more express than ever in his affections to him, and freeness wth him.

He had indeed a very happy & rare composure of sweetness and sollidity ; would play and dally wth ye king as if he were a woman ; and yet enquire & apprehend & argue councels & debates of state, as if a Burleigh or a Walsingham. He saw clearly that the affections of ye king were fading, wch the Puritans though never so much his friends could not repaire. He, therefore, eyed & adored ye rising sun, who now was growne

The Duke of Buckingham's temper.

growne & fit for marriage, and yet made no preparatives to find a Consort for him. He knew ye Spanish match was but a couler and a treaty dandled betweene Bristol and King James, to foole the Prince off, & shut his eares against the French proposals. This he discovers to the Prince, & tels him y^t Kings did not love an heyre apparent, how neere soever; that the daughter of Spaine was designed to a monastery, and kept in reserve for the Howse of Austria; that in France there was a lady much before her, and, if he pleased, he would wayt upon him into Spaine in a disguise, & take the French court in their way, & see that Lady, & so discover Bristol's & his Father's jugling. The Prince resents, and hugs the overture; they tell King James, that the Earl of Bristoll and the Spanish ministers abased him; that it was tyme to bringe that treaty to a conclusion, and desire they might goe into Spaine & play the game out.

The

The King saw who had ploughed wth his heyfer, & feared (as he was apt to doe) a cheque-mate; yet for the present urgeth only his affections to them both, and asketh how he should subsist so long wthout their companies. But they p̄sisting, the King signes a warrant wth his owne hand, for Jack Smyth, and Tom Smyth, wth each of them a servant & their horses, to goe beyond sea.

The Duke, even now, was not unmyndfull of D^r. Preston; and, therefore, leaves order wth ye Duchess, & Countess of Denbigh, to be carefull for him; & Sir Ralph Freeman, having a child to baptize, Doct^r Preston is intreated for to preach. The Dutchess & Countess were both gossips, who shewed to the D^r. very great respect, & gave him hopes of doing good; & some good he did; for he procured by their meanes Master Hildersham's liberty, & restitution to his place at Ashby De La Zouch; and

gave

gave great hopes unto good ministers of fairer tymes than had bin formerly. Only he would relate, with much regret, that he often found D^r. Lawd, then Bishop of St. David's, wth the Dutchess and Countess, & therefore doubted of ye issue & event.

The Doctor saw, by the debates about the Lecture, that he had enimyes as well as freinds at Court. He knew that the Duke was mutable as well as mortal; also that the King abhorred that journey into Spaine, & would remember it if able; "Dulcis inexperto, cultura potentis amici, expertus metuit." Therefore, though now he was settled & assured in the University, yet would he not leave his lecture at Lincoln's Inn; but, being still in London in the Terme tyme about the College business, continued preacher at Lincoln's Inn, and thought it might be a good reserve in case the naughty heads or factions

in

in the court should fall upon him. It was well he did this, for the Prince & Duke retorned the next Octobr highly offended wth ye Spanish gravity, & both they & all their traine did nothing but tell stories of the Spanish baseness. So a Parliamt was called, & the Duke was cryed up by all the Godly p̄ty in the kingdome. The Spanish agent at the Court had order from his master, out of Spaine, for to defy him, & protest against him at the Councell table ; but, seriously, he could not have done him a greater courtesy, for the people did universally hate ye Spaniard, and now he became the people's martyr. I have seen verses made in his defence & comendation. And now Agents were presently dispatched into France to treate of that match.

King James liked not this stuffe, but the Prince was able now to goe alone, especially having the Duke for one of

his

his supporters. All thinges now are fairely carried for Religion, as represented by the Duke of Buckingham's, the Prince's and the people's favourite. The people seemed now to have the better, & ye Court affaires for to declyne and droop. D^r. Preston, like another Mordecai, was very great, for the Prince was his master, & the Duke his friend ; and ye courtiers had their eyes upon him, because they saw he came not thither for preferment, as all men else did. His honours altered nothing in him, but gave encouragem^t to all the godly p̄ty, & his sermons at Lincoln's Inn much wrought upon the Parliament. A bold petition was now contrived & presented to the King at Whitehall, from both Houses of Parliam^t, April 1624, against the spreading & encrease of Popery, & the Indulgence given unto Priests and Jesuits.

King James was in the evening of his glory,

glory, his party in yᵉ Court under a clowd, another sun almost in vieu, and the daystar already risen. Therefore accordingly, he answered warily to their petition, bewayled his want of information as to the reall ground of this their trouble, wᶜʰ otherwise he had prevented; acknowleged that whilest the treaty lasted wᵗʰ Spaine & Austria he was obliged to comply, but now both being broken off, he would be rigid & severe against yᵉ Priests & Jesuits. He bids them finde out a way to restreyne the growth of Popery, and he would second them. But resolves secretly he would pay the Duke of Buckingham for all this; and gives order to the Earle of Bristoll to prepare an information for that end. Howsoever the match wᵗʰ France, & other intervenient accidents obstruct the King's designs for yᵉ present.

The Duke, having told tales out of schoole

schoole, & broken off ye match wth Spaine, was much obleiged to further & promote ye French ; wch he did seriously excuse to D^r. Preston, upon this ground, that there was not a Protestant to be had, and to marry wth a subject had always bin unhappy and fatall to ye Kings of England. He also argued that the French would not be so rigid in religious observations. The D^r., however, constantly opposed, only acknowledged this difference, that Spanish Popery was an absolute ingredient to their intended Western Monarchy, but French was not so, &, in so much, was less evill.

The French, on their part, found out how the land lay, & were untractable, unless the Duke would ayde the King of France against the Rochellers. This was a hard chapter for one so much obleiged to the Puritans ; therefore, he declyned all he could ; but nothing would serve. The Duke knew King James

James lay ready to take advantages; so, in conclusion, eight shipps were granted to oppose the Rochell Fleete; & many colours were sought to clowd it, & hide it from the world. But from that tyme Dr. Preston doubted of ye saintship of ye Duke of Buckingham, whom otherwise he honoured and loued very much. It was truly high tyme for the Duke to looke about him, for King James was not to learne now how to play his game; he was an old, but not a foolish king, Eccles. 4. 13. and, therefore, fayled not to lay rods in brine, that he might use upon occasion.

The Duke betrays ye Rochell-ers.

Kings used for to account an ague in the Spring their physique, yet physique till March be past is not good; but this ague of which we treat antidates the months, & comes in February. The King was then at Theobalds, and the ague which attacked him was made but small account of. He feared death, but

was

was the most impatient and disordered
of any living man, for what rules soever
the Physitians gave he would observe
none; wch intemperance might well oc-
cation the growing strength & vigour of
the disease; and, in good truth, it more
& more encreased, & at last began to
be considerable; he now began to take
advise, & to submit to rules; but then
it was too late; for March 27. 1625, on
the Lord's Day, the King dyed. D^r.
Preston then attended in his month,
and was sometimes hastened to the
Prince to comfort him, and sometimes
to the Duke; and indeed it was a very
mournfull morning. Death is a very
serious thinge, & knocks alike at Pal-
laces as at the meanest cottage.

King James was very much beloued
of all his servants; some of the hunts-
men could not be gotten from him.
The Prince and Duke were both of them
retyred, & wept exceedingly. And now
S^r

Sʳ Edward Conway & some of the Lords drew up a writing, & proclaymed Charles Steward King, wᵗʰ all his titles ; and hast was made to pack away to London. The Prince, & Duke, & Dʳ. Preston, in coaches shut downe, hasten to Whitehall ; & there the Prince is proclaymed againe, wᵗʰ more formallityes ; & the Lord Maior & yᵉ Citty sent to, where the proclamation was done wᵗʰ much solemnity, & great rejoycing of the people ; for the Prince had that exceeding happiness as to come upon the stage unprejudiced ; for he had never interposed or acted but in the Spanish business, and that succeeded to his great advantage ; so that if he listed he might have been as popular as ever any were.

This occasions many alterations in Court ; the Bishops, generally, and Doctʳ Preston's enimyes, and all that had contended wᵗʰ the Duke, were crestfallen. King James was like enough
to

to have outlived the Duke of Buckingham, who had bin very sick since his
retorne from Spaine; but all is altered,
& y* Duke doth all.

But he had many thinges to doe; the
affronts received at Madrid & at the
councel table by the agent, were to
be sent back by a puissant & mighty
navy, & provisions made accordingly;
King James to be interred; a Parliament to be summoned; the French
Lady to be sent for, & brought into
England; wch the Duke especially intended, & spake to all the gallants of
his retinue to attend him; & to many
others of ye gentry & nobillity throughout the kingdome; but he found it
hard thus in the morning of the King's
affaires to be abroad; there being then
a Parliament, & the sickness much encreasing in ye City; so he was constreyned to employ the Earle of Hol-
land, and attend himselfe at home.

All

All were not gratified in this great
Revolution & mutation of affaires; &
the discontented p̄ty murmured, & let
fly at the Duke; &, the sickness much
encreasing, began to make a mutiny.
It was much desired that the Parliament might be prorogued till some
other more healthfull & less dangerous
tyme; but the Navy against yᵉ Spani-
ards, and the pressing wants of all
sortes that depended on the court would
not p̄mit, so it was only adjourned to
Oxford, yet there yᵉ sickness was as
soone as they, & some of their members
smarted for it; but hast was made to
gratify the new King, and the provisions for the navy went forward, many
men engaged, and the King resolved
to attend that business as admitting
no delay.

There was one thinge that invited
Dr. Preston to a journey that yeare,
and that was a strong suspition that
yᵉ

yᵉ plague was in Cambridge, in wᶜʰ case there is a liberty to dissolve the college wᵗʰout any detriment to the officers & members of it; he was not willing to omit the opp͇tunity because he had many invitations into the West. The Bishop of Salisbury he desired to consult withall, about a booke of Mʳ. Montague's that was comended to him by yᵉ Duke of Buckingham to p͞use, & give him his sense upon it.

Mʳ. Chervil, the Recorder of Salisbury, was a Bencher of Lincoln's Inn, and a very good friend of his; he had also divers friends at Dorchester, & was desirous to be sea-sick, & was still inticed forward; and at last resolved to wait upon yᵉ King & Duke at Plymouth, whither they were gone to see the navy set sayle. Whilst he was there, the Rochell fleete was broaken by those ships the King lent, & Mounseiur Sabeeza came into Falmouth wᵗʰ the remainder,

mainder, & thence to Plymouth, wth
most lamentable outcries against the
Duke; who seemed to be very much
affected wth it, and made mighty promises of wonderfull repaires. But D^r.
Preston fayled not to set that business
home, he did beleeve the Duke was
overruled to send them, and sorry when
he saw ye sad effects.

But while the Duke was thus deteyned
in the west, the Earle of Bristol, and y^e
Lord Keeper Williams combined against
him, and drew in many to their p̄ty;
amonge others ye Earle of Pembrooke,
& divers great ones in ye Howse of
Commons; and were so encouraged &
heartned in it, that ye Earle of Bristol,
May 1. 1626, preferred in the Howse
of Com̄ons twelve articles against the
Duke of Buckingham; tending to prove
that the Duke had promised unto the
Pope & minister of Spaine, to make
the King a Papist, & overrule him
against

against the judgement of the Earle of Bristol ; to write unto the Pope wth the title of " Sanctissime Pater ;" that his carriage in matters of religion was such, that he stucke not to kneele before the Host, as often as he met it ; that he was so licentious and unchaste in his behaviour, that the Spanish ministers resolved not to have anythinge to doe wth him ; that when he could not bring about the match to his owne p̅ticcular advantage, he used means to obstruct it and breake it off ; that he (the Earl of Bristol) had informed King James of these thinges, who promised to heare him, & to leave the offender to justice ; and that not many dayes before his sickness.

The Duke had now reason to looke about him, and was very able so to doe ; first he labours to divide the p̅ty by drawing off of ye Earle of Pembrook, by promising his daughter to the Earle of

of Montgomerye's son ; wᶜʰ afterwards
he did accomplish; then he endeavoured
to obleige yᵉ Puritans by gratifying
of Dʳ. Preston all the wayes he could ;
& p̄ticcularly in the college suite, by
depriving Bishop Williams of yᵉ seale,
& giving it to Sʳ Thomas Coventry,
who was one of yᵉ college Councell ;
yea, he went so farr as to nominate
the Doctor to be Lord Keeper ; & the
King was so firme to him, that the
Earl of Bristol could doe no good, and
so wᵗʰdrew his articles.

Dʳ. Preston's friends were newters all
this while, & looked on, neither engaged for him, nor against him ; wᶜʰ
was sadly represented to the Duke by
the Bishop and that p̄ty, who woundred
that he should doate upon a man that
either could not or would not owne
him in his neede ; bad him consider
whether Puritans were like to be his
friends, whose wayes were " toto cælo "
                                    different ;

different; and told him plainly he could not have them both; if he adhered to those that sought their ruyne, they must adhere to those as would support them ; so that the Duke was in a great strait, & knew not what to doe.

D^r. Preston also was importuned to put it to an issue, and if the Duke would not leave the rotten and corrupted clergy, then to leave him; and because there had bin information against that booke of M^r. Montague's, they propounded it might come to a debate, and not remaine, as now it did, unsetled.

The Doctor & ye Duke were both of them unwilling to open a breach ; loued to temporize & wayt upon events ; but D^r. Preston's friends, would not be satisfied, but urged a conference; whereunto they were encouraged by some orthodox & very learned Bishops ; and
at

at last it was concluded, by two religious noblemen, that a conference there should be; the Bishop of Rochester, & Dr. White, then Deane of Carlile, on the one side; and the Bishop of Coventry & Lichfield & Dr. Preston on the other; a day was set, a Saturday in Hillary Terme at 4 of ye clock in the afternoone, the place was York Howse, & Dr. Preston sent to in the morning to attend it.

The noblemen came to the Bishop's lodgings about two of the clock; who sent for Dr. Preston to them, who gave many reasons why he could not goe; but they were resolute, &, taking ye Bishop wth them, went without him; but the Dr. considering, & fearing his absence might betray the cause, & give encouragement unto the other side, went afterwards himselfe unto the place, & sat by as a hearer silent, untill all was done.

But,

But, talking afterwards occasionally of falling from grace, the Bishop shewed that a Godly man might goe farr & yet retorne, by the instance of ye prodigal, Luke 15. But Doctor White exclaimed against any that should think the prodigall in acts of drunkenness & whoredome not to be fallen from Grace; and urged that of Rom. 1. 23. that those that doe such things are worthy of death; that is, said he, in a state of everlasting death, &, therefore, fallen from grace. So, 1 Cor. 6. 9. 10. shall not inherit the kingdome of God; that is, are not sons, for if sons, then heyres, Rom. 8. 17.

But D^r. Preston answered, that those sins indeed made a forfeiture of their interest into the hands of God, & He might take ye seysure if He pleased; yet did not unto those that were His children & in covenant wth Him; as two tenants, not paying of their rent, or keeping

keeping covenants, forfeited their leases;
yet the Lord might seize the one, and
not yᵉ other, as He pleased. But the
Bishop & the Deane both cryed that
this was the way to all licenciousness
& looseness; to wᶜʰ the Dᵣ. answered,
that the seed of God, as the apostle
calls it, 1 Joⁿ 3. 9. remained in the
sinning saint or son, & would repaire
him; as in water there remains a principle of cold even when it boyleth over,
that will undoubtedly reduce it when
the heate & fire is removed; as in
Peter, David, Sampson, & others was
apparent, so that they could not run
out into all licenciousness, for the spirit
lusted against yᵉ flesh, that they cannot doe the thinges they would, Gal.
5. 17.

He did not disinherit them, and blot
their names out of the Booke of Life,
Phil. 4. 3. yet He might & would
withdraw His favᵣ & imbitter all their
comforts,

comforts, Mat. 26. 75. raise troubles to them from their dearest interests, 2 Sam. 12. 11. and fill them wth anguish; Psal. 38. 3. 4. wch in reason will keep them from running out, seeing the evil is comēnsurable unto that good of pleasure or profit their sinn afforded; and, if neede be, He can add unto it eternall apprehensions, and make them feele the feirceness of His anger, Psal. 88. 6. 7. w^thout any hope of being eased; and after this can restreine & w^thhold them, as he did Abimilech, Gen. 20. 6. For, if one cease to be a sonne because he comīts a sin that doth deserve eternall death, Rom. 6. 23. and because in many thinges we offend all, James 3. 2. we should be always out of sonshipp, & have neither certeinty nor comfort in our estate; unless he could give some ground out of Scripture to assure what sinnes puts us out & what doth not.

The Duke had sent to Doctor Preston

ton to decline this clashing conference, and assured him that he was as much his friend as ever, & would have stopt it if he could, but the Bishops had overruled it; wch the D^r. at first beleeved, and so was backward ; but when he saw the confidence of D^r. White and his companion, he doubted the sincerity of that assurance; and was afterwards informed that there had bin a meeting at the Countess of Denbigh's, & the Duke had promised to leave him. This gave him resolution & encouragement against the second conference, wch was managed in a manner by him alone against M^r. Montague & D^r. White; for when the D^r. saw that ye Duke doubled wth him, he was less fearefull to offend him ; though the Duke still carried it wth all ye faireness he could, & appeared not in p̄son.

The Duke sends to the D^r. to declyne to dispute against severall of ye Bishops y^t were Arminians.

When the time came for the second conference, the D^r readily appeared ; and

The D^r.s resolve to dispute notwithstanding.

and the first thing he charged M^r.
Montague with was his Doctrine of
Traditions, wch he affirmed he had delivered as grossly & erroniously as any
Papist. Gag. Page 38. 39. 40. For he justified that place in Bazil, where he
saith the Doctrine retained in ye Church
was delivered, p̄tely by written instructions, p̄tely by unwritten traditions,
having both a like force unto piety.
W^{ch} was so unlike unto Bazil, and the
opinions of those tymes, that it was
generally beleeved to be put in by the
Papists of later tymes.

Master Montague confessed it was
suspected by some of ye preciser cut;
but D^r. Preston told him that Bishop
Bilson was none of them, yet he did
judge it supposititious; & it must be so,
or else Bazil acknowledged to be erro-
nious; moreover, he instanced the pray-
ing towards the East, & the use of
Crisme or oyle in baptisme; both w^{ch}
being

being rejected by the Church of England, argues that the Church holds y^t place in Bazil not canonical.

Master Montague answered, that the sense of the assertions there used by S^t. Bazil might signify that some thinges that seemed true, albeit of less esteeme & consequence, might be delivered by tradition; as long as matters more substantiall were taken from ye Scriptures. But D^r. Preston shewed that the assertions signified oftentimes doctrine, and were used heere by Bazil to denote those heads of doctrine that were more principle & less exposed, comparing them unto those places in the Temple, whereunto the people had not access. Master Montague answered further that his assertion was hypothetical, and that if a doctrine came from the same authour it was no great matter whether it were by writing or word of mouth, for either had ye same authority. But D^r.
Preston

Preston told him that Bazil was positive, and spake directly, and therefore could not be hypotheticall, as he pretended.

It is a great step unto victory for to divide; Paul sets ye Pharisees against the Saduces, Acts 23. 7. 8. that he might save himselfe.   The Jesuits are so good at it, that though they have but one to be their adversary, they endeavour to divide him from himselfe, by moving passion, or compassion, or some affection of his owne against him.   D^r. White had openly in the Commencement Howse mainteyned that election is not "ex prævisis operibus," and therefore D^r. Preston resolved to pintch M^r. Montague in that p̄ticcular, that he might bereave him of his animating champion D^r. White.

Severall passages recited by the D^r. in M^r. Montague's Booke.

There were fower severall places that D^r. Preston had observed to make good his charge: the first wch he produced was

was Gag. Page 179. Some Protestants
hold that Peter was saved, because God
would have it so, wthout respect unto
his faith & obedience ; and Judas
damned, because God would have it
so, wthout respect unto his sin ; and
ironically added, "this is not ye doctrine
of the Protestants, this is not the doctrine of the church, the church of England hath not taught it, doth not beleeve
it, hath opposed it." Now D^r. White,
who was very fierce & eager to engage,
told him it was no doctrine of the church
of England, but a private fancy of some,
that Judas was condemned wthout respect unto his sin ; for the wages of sin
is death, Rom. 6. 23. the soule that sin-
neth shall dye, Ezek. 18. 4.

But D^r. Preston answered he did not
charge that upon M^r. Montague, but the
former $\overline{pte}$ of y^e assertion, that Peter
was not saved wthout respect unto his
beleeving & obedience, & so election
should

should not be absolute, but grounded
on faith & workes foreseene. Then,
saith D^r. White, I have nothing against
that, but leave M^r. Montague to answer
for himselfe.

D^r. Preston was glad that he was eased
of D^r. White, & yet resolved to make
advantage of it ; and, therefore, told D^r.
White, if he thought election was not
" ex fide prævisâ," he desired to know
whether saving grace were an effect, or
fruit, of election or no ? D^r. White readily
acknowledged it was. Then said D^r.
Preston, whosoever hath saving grace
is elected ; now you know that an elect
p̅son can never finally miscarry, or fall
away, therefore, whosoever hath true
grace can never fall away.

The old man saw the snare & would
have avoyded it by denying the consequence ; but the D^r. urged that whereso-
ever ye effect is, there must be ye cause ;
but

but saving grace is an effect of election.
This D^r. White would have denyed ; but
the hearers murmured that the effect
could not be wthout the cause, as the
day could not be without the presence
of the sun.

Then D^r. White answered that saving grace was an effect indeed, yet
but a comon effect.   D^r. Preston urged
that it was not more comon than elec-
tion, for all the elect had saving grace,
& none but they ; and, therefore, they
could never fall away ; but this, said
he, is by the way, I will now apply my-
selfe to M^r. Montague.

But when M^r. Montague pceived that
D^r. White, his great Goliah, forsooke him,
he was greatly troubled, & cavilled at
the words awhile ; but, the booke ad-
judging it for D^r. Preston, he said that
the church of England had not declared
any thinge against it.   D^r. Preston al-
ledged

K

ledged the 17th Article, and told' M^r. Montague that he affirmed the church of England did oppose it.

But after one of ye Lords whispered wth M^r. Montague, he confessed, as for Arminius, he had never read him; and that he had writ some thinges negligently in that booke; wch he never thought would have bin so scanned amonge friends; and therefore promised to write another booke in butter & honey, and therein more exactly for to acquit him-selfe.

Some of ye Lords proposed that, in-stead of this booke wch M^r. Montague promised to write, the Synod of Dort might be received & established as the doctrine of the church of England, see-ing there was nothing there determined but what our delegates approved. But D^r. White opposed this mainly; for, said he, the church of England, in her chata-chisme,

chisme, teacheth to beleeve in God yᵉ Son, who redeemed me and all man-kinde, wᶜʰ that Synod did deny.

Dʳ. Preston answered, that by redemption there was only meant the freeing of mankind from that inevitable ruine the sin of Adam had involved them in, and making them savable upon conditions of another covenant. Joⁿ 3. 16. 17. So that now salvation was not impossible, as it was before the death of Christ; but might be offered unto any man, according to the tenour of that commission, Mark 16. 15. 16. This could not however be applied unto the Divels, for they were left in that forlorne condition whereinto their sin & disobedience put them, Heb. 2. 16. & 2 Pet. 2. 4. On the other hand, the jaylor, Acts 16. 24. 27. was a boysterous, bloody fellow, yet Paul made no doubt to tell him, verse 31. that, if he beleeved in the Lord Jesus, he should be saved

wᵗʰ

wth his howse. But D^r. White would in no sorte admit this, but affirmed earnestly that Christ dyed for all alike in God's intention and decree ; for Cain as well as Abel ; for Saul as well as David ; for Judas as much as Peter ; for the reprobate & damned in Hell as well as for the elect and saints in Heaven.

To which D^r. Preston answered, that there was a speciall salvation offered to beleevers, 1 Tim. 4. 10. That Christ was indeed a ransome for all, 1 Tim. 2. 6. yet the Saviour only of his body, Ephes. 5. 23. That he redeemed all, but called, justified, & glorified, whom he knew before, & had predestinated to be formable to ye image of his son, Rom. 8. 29. 30. That to whom in this sense Christ was given, to them were given also all things appteyning unto life & Godlyness, 2 Pet. 1. 3. As faith, 2 Pet. 1. 1. Phil. 1. 29. Ephes. 2. 8. Repentance,

Repentance, Acts 11. 18. 2 Tim. 2. 25.
A new heart, Ezek. 36. 26. His Spirit,
Gal. 4. 5. 6. So that nothing can be
charged on them, Rom. 8. 31. 32. 33.
34. So that they can never perish
nor be taken out of Christ's hand, Jon
10. 28. 29. 30. But as they are begot-
ten again unto a lively hope, 1 Pet. 1. 3.
so they are kept by the power of God
through faith unto salvation, verse 5.
Whereas Judas was lost, Jon 17. 12. and
is gone to his owne place, Acts 1. 25.

And there are many nations & people
of ye world, that have no outward offer
made unto them in ye Gospel, Psal. 147.
19. 20. Acts 16. 6. 7. And those that
enjoy ye meanes of grace, have not all
hearts given them to understand & beleeve it, Deut. 29. 2. 3. 4. Isaiah 6. 9. 10.
Mat. 13. 13. 14. 15. and therefore they
are lost, 2 Cor. 4. 3. 4. and are damned.
2 Thess. 2. 10. 11. 12. He shewed
them, in Adam all men were lost, Rom.
5. 12.

5. 12. and none recovered but by Christ ;
therefore, such as had not Christ's inter-
cession could not recover ; That Christ
prayed but for some, Joⁿ 17. 9. and
therefore none but such only could be
saved, Heb. 9. 15.

D^r. White acknowledged there was a
difference ; for, though all had so much
as by good improvement might serve
their turne, yet the elect had more, for
God abounded towards them, Ephes. 1.
8. 9. Rom. 5. 15. 17. 20.   Thus, by
example, all the troope have horses,
but the officers have better ; two travel-
lers have staves to leape over a ditch,
yet ye one a stronger & better than y^e
other ; the worst men had grace enough
to keepe corruption & the evil of their
nature downe, but the elect such as
would doe it easily.   Christ had tasted
death for every man; Heb. 2. 9. he
dyed for those who might notwithstanding p̄rish, 1 Cor. 8. 11. and bought those
that

that yet might bring upon themselves swift damnation, 2 Pet. 2. 1. because they did not husband & improve ye favour offered to them.

D^r. Preston answered that Christ was in himselfe sufficient to save all ; and might be said to be provided for that end & use; as a medicine is to cure infected p̄sons, though it cures none actually but those that drinke it. " Habet in se quod omnibus prosit, sed, si non bibitur, non," as in 1 Joⁿ 5. 11. 12. But many did not thus apply Christ, because they had him not so offered & exhibited as others had, Mat. 11. 21. Luke 10. 13. for God gave some faith & repentance, as I have shewed. The serpent (Moses was commanded to make), was in itselfe sufficient to cure those that were bitten, Numb. 21. 8. 9. yet cured none but only those who looked on it. " So, as Moses lifted up the Serpent in the wilderness, shall the Son of Man be lifted

lifted up, that whosoever beleeved in Him should not perish but have everlasting life," John 3. 14. 15.

D^r. White urged that place, Esay. 5. 4. that God had done all he could, but they neglected and rejected the councell of God against themselves, Luke 7. 30.

D^r. Preston answered, that God had done all that they could challenge of Him, for he had given them in Adam power to be upright, Eccles. 7. 29. and proposed another way in a Mediator; and therefore excuseth his judgment, Isaiah 5. 3. Yet this was then offered unto Israel only; "he had not delt so with any other nation," Psal. 147. 19. 20. Besides he had done what he could, wthout reversing & rescinding his decree, Jo^n 12. 38. 39. 40; for otherwise he could have given them "the same spirit of faith," 2 Cor. 4. 13. "The like guift that

that he did unto others who beleeved
in the Lord Jesus," Acts 11. 17. he could
have "wrought in them both to will &
to doe of his good pleasure," Phil. 2. 13.
He could have healed them as he promised, Isa. 57. 18. and as he did p̄sc-
cuting Paul, Acts 9. 17. 18. But God
had other ends, Rom. 9. 17. and attributes, Rom. 9. 22. wᶜʰ he was willing
to discover, Prov. 16. 4.

But Dʳ. White asked, how then God
could require faith & repentance ? Mark
1. 15. Acts 17. 30. Which was all one
as if any should desire a man to give
his judgement or opinion of a coulor
that had his eyes shut, and then shut
his eyes as fast as he could.

Dʳ. Preston answered that God might
doe it to shew and discover our impo-
tency ; just so as we bid our little children to rise, that by their owne fault
fell, in order to let them know their
owne

owne inabillity, & that they may be the more beholding to us to help them up, as Mark 9. 23. 24. And, because the call & comand of Christ is the vehiculum & conduit pipe of strength & power, Acts 14. 10. Jo^n 5. 8. 9. & Jo^n 11. 43. 44. thus God, by bidding men & comanding them to take Grace, doth thereby fit and enable them ye more to doe it. As y^t creeple, Acts 3. 6. 7. 8. was by y^o comand enabled; also Saul (afterwards called Paul), being comanded to receive his sight, was enabled the same moment to looke upon Ananias, Act 22. 13. who, vers. 16. being comanded to wash away his sins, had the blood of Christ provided ready for to doe it. These comands are not like those the apostle speakes of, James 2. 16. but heere is something given. When God bids He doth not "verba dare sed rem."

But D^r. White further urged that God

had

had no pleasure in the death of wicked men, Ezek. 33. 11. but much rather that they would repent & leave their sinnes, Ezek. 18. 23. 32. If God, therefore, were not ready to the utmost of his power to give them grace, he could not be excused from dissembling & double dealing.

To wᶜʰ Dr. Preston answered, that superiours may comand unable p̄sons for many reasons, yet cannot be said to dissemble, unless they refuse to give when the required condition is p̄formed. As, if I bid one come unto me & I will give him sixpence, then if I refuse when he is come I do dissemble, but, if he comes not, he cannot chardge me; for his not coming may be for want of will, Joⁿ 5. 40. as well as for want of power, Joⁿ 6. 44. And if I know a creeple will not come though he could, I may punish him for it.

It's

It's true God delights in nothing but Himselfe; His joy & comfort is teriminated in Himselfe; not in the creature, but as He is in some way served & represented by it; for God made all thinges for Himselfe, Prov. 16. 4. yea for His pleasure, Rev. 4. 11. That is for ye exercise & illustration of some one of His attributes; as His power, Exod. 9. 16. Rom. 9. 17. His wrath, Rom. 9. 22. Never did strong man glory of his strength more than God doth of His soveraignty & omnipotency, Job 40. 9. 10. 11. 12. 13.

Now, if it fall but that, in the illustration & exercise of those his glorious attributes & excellencyes, some creatures smart, yet he delights not in their smart & sufferings, but in ye demonstration of his omnipotency. Ahasuerus makes a feast to all the estates & orders of his kingdome, to show the riches of his glorious kingdome, and ye honour of his excellent

excellent Majesty, Hest. 1. 3. 4. This was not done wthout the smart & suffering of many of ye creatures; yet he delighted not in their sufferings, but in his owne magnificence & bounty. When Christ was at the feast, Joⁿ 2. 1. 2. he doth condole the death of those innocents that went to make it, yet rejoyced in the good cheere & good will of ye friend that bade him.

There were few present of D^r. Preston's friends; &, accordingly, this conferrence was represented & reported wth all the disadvantage that could be to him; insomuch, that many Parliament men that were his friends were much offended at it. This occasioned D^r. Preston, as soone as he came to Cambridge, to write the severall passages of his disputation, & send them to those friends that were unsatisfied. This was all an evidence that ye Duke & Doctor Preston were not so great friends as before, but that

that the Duke sticked to the Prelats,
and would, in yᵉ issue, leave Dʳ. Preston
& the Puritans; wᶜʰ much abated many
men's affections to the Duke. It was
beleeved at the same time that he had
no such interest in yᵉ King's affections
as he pretended to. They thought his
greatness began to languish, and it was
beleeved in the University that there
was another favourite in being, though
yet obscure.

The Earle of Suffolke much about this
tyme dyed, who had bin a long tyme
Chancellor of yᵉ University of Cambridge. Great means was used to get yᵉ
Duke up to succeed him; but many men
were fallen off because of his deserting
Dʳ. Preston, and others did beleeve his
glory was depted. The Earle of Berk-
shire, therefore, the former Chancellor's
second sonne, was set up against the
Duke, and many voted for him that
loved greatness, and were servants unto
the

the tymes, and it is beleeved it had
bin carried for him against the Duke, if
the wisedome of Dr. Goffing, then Vice
Chancellor, and some others who super-
intended the scrutiny, had not prevented
it. So it was pronounced for the Duke,
& great care was taken for the investing
of him in a very sollemne manner.

Representatives of ye University were
designed to attend him at Yorke Howse,
in their habits, and a sumptuous feast
provided for their enterteinment. The
Duke sate in the middle of the table
amonge the Doctors ; where (by some-
body) there was a health begun unto ye
King. When it came to Dr. Preston for
to pledge it, he was uncovered & bowed
as others had done, but drunk but very
little, & so delivered it unto the next ;
but one of ye Doctors tooke notice that
he drunck not all ; and told him he had
seene him drinke as great a glass of
wine, & did beleeve he could have
drunke

drunke this if he would, but he loved to be singular. The D^r. acknowledged he was not skilfull in ye lawes of drinking healths, &, therefore, if he had offended, desired it might be imputed to his ignorance. He said he thought the end was to shew respect unto ye p̄son named; wch was done best by the ceremonyes that preceded, such as being bare, standing up, & such like; wherein he sayd he had not willingly offended. But, if it were an engine to court intemperance, & to engage men unto greater quantityes than themselves liked, it fell short of that modesty & temperance of the heathens, Esther 1. 8. and was a sin in all; but, in men of their degree & ranke, an abominable wickedness.

The Duke misliked this incivillity, & frowned on the Doctor that occasioned it; but, it was beleeved it could not have bin done w^thout assurance that the Duke's affections were ebbing towards D^r.

D^r. Preston. And no wonder, for, his end being to make impressions of good upon the court, he could not but see that if they did not succeed they would recoyle. If you manure & sow yor land, if ye seed subdue it not & conquer it, it is enabled to bring forth ye stronger weeds, Heb. 6. 7. 8. If you cast pearles before swyne they will turne againe & rend you, Mat. 7. 6.

The Duke had now seen ye worth & way of D^r. Preston; he had found that he could not win him & make him his; he could not, therefore, in a way of policy, but labour & resolve to wrack & sinke him. When Herod was called to account by the conquering Augustus, for the great assistance he had given to Marke Anthony his adversary, and knew it would be in Augustus' power to take off his head, he setled his affaires; but gave premptory order that his beloved Marianne should be put to death, for this

this only reason, because another should not enjoy so great a beauty. So the Duke would not another should enjoy the great abillityes of D^r. Preston, but was resolved to breake him if he could, yet in a civil court way.

But the D^r. was too knowing not to see this afarr off, Prov. 22. 3. and had accordingly provided a succession of reserves wherein to hide himselfe. The first and surest was his conscience, 2 Cor. 1. 12. "This is our rejoycing, the testimony of our conscience, that in simplicity & Godly sincerity, not wth fleshly wisedome but by the grace of God, we have had our conversation in the world." If a man be welcomb to his conscience, he needs not feare ye storms & blusters that he meets abroad. When a man is forced to be where he would not, as Peter was foretold he should be, Joⁿ 21. 18. yet he may, in despight of them, retire into himselfe.

Paul

Paul made it his business to have his conscience always voyd of offence, Acts 24. 16. and so did D^r. Preston; for his actings (being many of them above the comon size) were not always understood, & very often misinterpreted; yet he was innocent & upright always in them. An undeniable argument whereof was that he never sued for the least preferment, as I have said, but studied & often consulted how, without breaking, he might avoyd them.

And, though he lived like himselfe, & gave releefe to others, yet it was ever of his owne, as very many yet alive can witness. Indeed he was a man of very much comunion & sweet society wth God; prayed much in private & by himselfe; besides as tutour with his pupils; & often as Master in his familly, whatever weakness he was in, or business did occur; kept many private days of fasting by himselfe, especially before

before yᵉ Sacrament & Sabbath days; and accordingly enjoyed a constant clearness & assurance of his justification, & interest in yᵉ blood of Christ. Even then when frailtyes & infirmityes did most of all afflict & wound him, he never, that I knew, was troubled or p̅plexed about adoption, though very often about the imp̅fection of his graces, and the unconstancy of sanctification; so as he studied most exactly that treatise of "the Sts. infirmityes," and there is nothing in all his works that may more prop̅ply be called his.

His next retreat was Lincoln's Inn; for now, he said, the Duke was Chancellor, & would endeavour to ingratiate himself & be a Benifactor; he had bought Erpenius' Manuscripts, and did verily intend to found a library; & so it would be easy & in his power to out him of yᵉ college & university; for there was a resolution of some of the fellows to petition

petition the Duke to annul ye statute of continuance or com͞moration in the college. Yet he conceived the lawyers would pretend a kind of freedome & exemption ; for he saw when that holy & blessed D^r. Sibbs was outed both of fellowship & Lecture in the university, yet by the goodness and prudence of S^r. Henry Yelverton, that constant patron unto Godly ministers (a virtue yet running in ye veins of his posterity), he was received & reteyned at Grey's Inn unto his death. Therefore, in no sort would he leave his title unto, and interest in, Lincoln's Inn ; but reserved it in his power unto his dying day.

Yet he knew the King had long hands, & y^t ye Duke's were nothing shorter, and that Lincoln's Inn, though a great deale stronger and better built then Gray's Inn, yet would not hold out long in case the Duke should seriously beleager it ; therefore, he considered

His re-
solve to
have gone
to Bazil.

sidered of removing further off if needs
were ; and, having weighed all retreats,
resolved upon Bazil, in the Switzers'
country, as a place wch ye longest handed
kings had seldome touched, even when it
was a receptacle of their greatest enimyes.
Therefore he resolved, in case he could
not be free in England, to settle there,
& spend ye residue of his surviving
dayes in writing what he was not suffered to preach, or had not published
according to his mynde.

He was naturally very affable and
courteous to strangers of any country, &,
conversing much wth them, endeavoured
to preserve his knowledge in ye French
& Italian languages. But, after he had
thus resolved upon Bazil, he was very
friendly to all ye Germans that were
dispersed from severall universityes, es-
petially from ye Palatinate; for whom
he procured severall sortes of entertein-
ments, both in ye country abroad & in
         y^e

yᵉ University; for wᶜʰ kindness he had many gratulatory epistles from p̄ticcular p̄sons, especially one of note from the King of Bohemia, under his hand & seale.

But he knew that these were but yᵉ foxe's earths, that might successively be taken and posessed; he, therefore, also thought upon that "Unum magnum" of the Holy Ghost, Prov. 18. 10. "the name of the Lord," that is the goodness, mercy, power of the mighty God; there he was well assured he should for ever be free from Kings & Dukes. Yet these did no way retard his industry in using meanes; obstructions quicken industrious & active myndes, but damp & clogg the dull. There is a statesman of no meane esteeme that writes professedly against the use of cittadels & forts, because it makes the souldier less resolute in engagements; and yᵉ Spartans were forbidden to wall their citty, because it would encourage cowardise.

cowardise. But it did not take off D^r. Preston from his duty, for finding that his standing at court was undermyned, he resolved upon buttresses to support him in ye country.

There was in the country of North-ampton a gentleman of very able p̄ts, & cleare affections to ye publique good, no stranger to ye court in former tymes, nor to ye Duke of Buckingham, wth whom ye Doctor used to comunicate affaires, and was then a Parliament man of much esteeme; to him the D^r., in a letter, discovers all, & showes him the hopeless posture of ye Duke; how much they both were disappointed in him; layes some directions what to doe, and urgeth activeness. This l̄r̄e, by a sad misfortune, was let fall by him that was intrusted to convey it, about Tem-ple Barr, & handed from one to another, untill it came to Sr Henry Spillers; who, having viewed it, & pondred ye contents, concluded

concluded it was a purchasse that would ingratiate him to yᵉ Duke, & so imediately presents it to him.

The Duke was troubled to read his faults & face so shrewdly intimated & presaged; his temper was exceeding good, & he could mannage his affections many tymes wᵗʰ much serenity & moderation; but now he was quite off, & could not thinke of anythinge but a revenge. I have not knowne anythinge so trouble the Dʳ. as this did, that yᵉ Duke should have his hand against him, & that he had involved so good a man to whom he wrote. But it pleased God to cut yᵉ Duke out other worke; for yᵉ cry of Rochel & yᵉ Protestants of France was so exceeding great, & so much resented by the Parliament, that the Duke resolves to vindicate his honour by releeving them. So, whilst he was busy to get that fleete out & furnish forces for surprising the Isle of Rhees, he could not undertake

take that worke of revenge against D^r. Preston.

But the D^r. thought he had not done enough unless he proclaymed in the pulpit what he had often told ye Duke in private, according to that comand of Christ, Mat. 6. 27. "What I tell you in darkness, that speake you in light, & what ye heare in ye eare, that preach on the howsetops;" as Chrysostom to his people, "cum verum singuli audire non vultis publice audietis." When the French match was concluded he preached y^t sermon "of the Ground & Piller of truth," against ye mingling of religions, & mixing truth wth falcehood, & shewed how impossible it was to mingle truth wth errour, or make up one religion of theirs & ours. For, should they leave but any tenent * of their Church, it would follow that ye Church in that before had erred,

---

* Tenet.

and

and so that Pillar would be overthrowne,
on wch hanged so many points of Popery.
Neither could we p̄te wth any one truth;
for religion is of that brittle nature,
breake it you may, bend it you cannot.
It cannot be accomodated to respects
of Policy, & interests of States & King-
doms; but, as elements, when mingled
in a compound body, doe loose their
prop̄p formes, so religions, when made
ingredients & compounding p̄ts of any
other, doe lose their formes, & cease
to be religions in God's account, 2 Kings
17. 33. 34. See "Pillar and Ground of
Truth," Page 16.

When the Rochellers in distress layd
their ruyne & disasters at our doores,
& fathered their losses & calamityes on
us, Dr. Preston preached that sermon
of "the new life," where, Page 48, we
have these wordes; "We cannot stand
alone, what measure we mete to others
in their distress men shall measure the
same

same to us in our necessity, Luke 6. 38. If any be an impediment, nay, if any doe not their best, I pronounce this in the name of ye most high true God, that shall make it good sooner or later, that they & their howse shall p̄rish," Esther 4. 14. The Court was hoodwinkt in all these cominations, for by " Church " they understood ye Prelates and their party ! The King thought that if he adhered to them, & did his work, he was absolved ; but those that have read ye comentaryes, that have since bin writ in red Letters, will have occasion to beleeve the contrary.

When the Duke was in the Isle of Rhee, in wch voyadge he had engaged many of his very good friends, & much of ye Nobillity & gentry of the king-dome, the Doctor preached that sermon, called "ye demonstration of ye Diety," upon Isa. 64. 4. where, Page 81. 82, you have these wordes. " It is certeine evil is intended against us, & will come upon us, except

except something be done to prevent it.
For there is a covenant betweene God &
us, & breach of covenant causeth a quarrell ; the quarrell of God shall not goe un-
revenged. He saith to the Isralits, Levit.
26. 25. " I will send a sword upon you that
shall revenge the quarrell of my covenant. As if he should say, There is
a covenant, and you have broake that
covenant, & therefore I have a quarrell,
& I will send a sword to avenge my
quarrell. Now the quarrels of God are
not rash & passionate as men's are ;
and, therefore, he will not lay them aside
w^{th}out some true & reall satisfaction."

" If we will not beleeve his word, yet
shall we not beleeve his actions? Hath
he not begun? Are we infatuated & see
nothing? Doe we not see the whole body
of those that profess the truth are be-
sieged round about through Christen-
dome? At this tyme, are not present
enemyes not only stirred up but united
together,

together, & we disjoyned to resist them? Are not our allies wasted? Are not many branches of the Church cut off already, & more in hazard? In a word, have not our enterprizes bin blasted, & withered under our hands for the most p̄te? Have not thinges been long going downe the hill, & are now even hastning to a period? And doe not we say now that such an accident, and such a miscarriadge of such a business, & such men, are the causes? But, who is the cause of these causes? Is it not he without whose Providence a sparrow falls not to the ground? Are not these cracks to give warning before the fall of the howse? Are not these the grey hayres wch Hosea speakes of, that are heere & there upon us, and we discerne them not? Gray haires you know are a signe of old age & approach unto death."

This sermon was preached to the King at Whitehall on the Lord's Day; and, on the

the Wensday following, the newes came
of the totall routing of our army in the
Isle of Rhees ; wᶜʰ was such a ratification
of his prediction but the Sabbath day
before, as made many beleeve he was
a Prophet ; and they called him Micaiah
because he seldome prophesied good
unto them. Dʳ. Neale, then Bishop of
Winchester, said that he talked like one
that was familliar wᵗʰ God Almighty ;
and they were the more affected wᵗʰ it
because the Dʳ. had another course to
preach before his month was out (for
every chaplin was to preach twice, once
upon yᵉ Lord's Day, and also upon the
Tewsday).

The Dʳ. was desirous to exchange
his course upon the Tuesday, for a sabbath day ; so Dʳ. Potter preached on
the Tewsday, & Dʳ. Preston was to preach
on the Lord's day following. He was
resolved to p̄ceed on the same text,
and to handle a point relating to the
third

third verse ; for having shewed in the
4th verse that thinges were not done
by chance, but by God, he now resolved
for to show that God did all thinges
that men doe not looke for.   W[ch] being
knowne amonge the Bp[s], and they af-
frighted wth that disaster of y[e] Isle of
Rhees, they interceded wth y[e] clerke
of the closset, that seeing D[r]. Preston's
turne was past already, and this was
D[r]. Potter's, another might be put up
and he deferred untill another tyme.
This was yielded to, and, upon the Friday
before, a messenger was sent unto the
D[r]. to tell him that another was provided to preach for D[r]. Potter, & he
might spare his paines.

The Doct[r] woundred at the Providence ;
for he was resolved fully to have said in
that sermon, if he had bin suffered, that
which would in reason have deserved Micaiah's enterteynment, 1 Kings 22. 27.
But God was mercifull to him, & used his
enimyes

enimyes as instruments to prevent yᵗ danger.

It would have damped some men to have bin thus refused; he might have said wᵗʰ him, Mat. 22. 4. "Behold I have prepared my dinner, my oxen & my fatlings are killed, & all things are ready;" but he considered what he had preached before, and that a sparrow fell not to the ground wᵗʰout God's will; that his desire & resolution for to sacrifice his all was accepted, as Abraham's was; that his sermon, whilst in embryo & only in intention, had an efficacious operation upon the auditory; for, as they had shewed and discovered their feares, so good men did their joyes; & the sermon was more talked of at Court & in the citty than any sermon that ever he had preached before; for all men enquired what yᵉ sermon was that Dʳ. Preston was not suffered to preach; and many wise men were p̄swaded that it did more good

good then it would have done in case it had bin preached so that, instead of being damped & dejected at the affront, he was enlivened & encouraged.

I never knew him come home from the court more satisfied then he did this tyme, nor more encouraged in his ministry at Cambridge ; for, he was then upon those sermons of the attributes of God that since were printed, and the Lord was greatly wth him in them.

Those Fellows at Emanuel, who had bin active in making of him Master there, were much satisfied, because the Doctor never would consent to the annulling of that statute, "De mora sociorum in Collegio;" for he was convinced that ye Founder had added it upon weighty grounds. He saw it was a meanes to make y^o fellows preach, & looke abroad, & less intend the actings of the master ; & that young schollars were heartned in their

their studyes, wth hopes y^t there would be preferments ready for them.

It was ordinary amonge the schollars to looke how long some fellows were to stay; therefore, observing these affronts at court, they petitioned the King that that statute might be abrogated. The Duke was glad upon this occasion to be revenged upon his old friend D^r. Preston, and did embrace it wth all alacrity. Commissioners were dispatched for to heare & consider the allegations ; and many meetings & debates were had about it. It was acknowledged that the statute was of equall power & vallidity wth the rest, though added three yeares after ; and upon that, one of ye fellows that had petitioned fell off.

The D^r. used all his friends for to support & keepe in power this statute, & found very many very forward to

assist

assist him in it ; but above all, a very noble grandchild of ye founder's, yet living, did much encourage and enable the defence ; who, though a courtier & much obleiged, yet did adventure and wave all his interests, rather than he would behold his grandfather's pious & prudent care so overthrowne. So a temper was at last agreed upon, that it should be suspended from effects in law, untill six Livings of a hundred pounds each p̄ annum should be annexed unto the college.

The soule is the undoubted soveraigne of ye body & hath therein an absolute & uncontrolled jurisdiction ; and, in case of injury or overburdening, there is no action lies. But soules should consider, "soft & faire goes farr." "Qui vult regnare diu, languida regnat manu." It was Hobson, the carier, that told the scholars they would come time enough to London if they did not ride too fast.

It

It was incurable in this good man to override himselfe; for when the body is tyred we cannot take a new one at the next stage as we doe horsses. But he thought all was one, some lived as much in seaven yeares as others did in seaventy, "Non diu vixit sed diu fuit" was his opinion of many men; he thought that our life is like iron that will consume wth rust as much as wth imployment.

These were his principles, and his actings were according; most unmercifull was he to his flesh of any living being, thinking that not tyme but action should be the metwand of all men's lives; "non annos meos, sed victorias numero." Not, how long I have lived, but how? God usually allows his dearest servants tyme to doe their worke in, Moses 120 yeares of age, Deut. 34. 7. David an old man before he dyes, 1 Cron. 29. 28. Paul, aged, Philemon 9. notwthstanding

ing all his labours & activity. But ye D^r. had a shorter period put unto his days. All men's is set, Job 7. 1. His was short. It was no disparagement to good Josiah to die about the D^{rs} age, 2 Cron. 34. 1. Our glorious King Edward, that scarce outlived his minority, outstript, notwthstanding, all his longest living prædecessors in doing good. God, who had set his time, hastened his service; and so he did the D^{rs}; his preaching & studying labours were exceeding great; but that wch spent & wore him was his cares & troubles for the Churche's safety & prosperity, & he would often inculcat upon 2 Cor. 11. 28. "That wch cometh upon me daily, the care of all ye churches."

When his body, therefore, began to be sick & languish he was content a little to abate, & take off, and thought a country howse in some good ayre might (as formerly it had done) advantage him.

him. He accordingly tooke one at Linton neere the hills, about 6 myles off, wᶜʰ he furnished, & purposed to be in all the weeke, and retorne on Saturdyes to preach on yᵉ Lord's dayes; and, had this course bin taken tyme enough, much might have bin done.

But now he feared that sollicitude would be turned into sollitude, and the ayre of sutable converse he doubted would be wanting there; and being alone, he saw would too much gratify his melancholly. The spring then approaching, he was willing to consult wᵗʰ some physicians; but London being farr off, he sent to Bury for Dr. Despotine. His present malady was want of rest, wᶜʰ now tobacco would not help him to as formerly, and, therefore, he proposed letting of blood. The Physician told him that it might p̄haps allay his heates & purchass sleepe, but, if he were wᵗʰin the verge of a consumption,

tion, it would be fatal to him ; notwithstanding which advise, ye deceitfull hopes of present ease inticed him, & so was let blood. He never lived to repaire that loss, &, sinking more & more, he went to London, & tooke advise of those who were best acquainted wth his state of health ; by their advise he retired a little into Newington, unto a loving friend of his that lived there, and then into Hertfordshire, a thinner & more peircing ayre.

The malady, they all agreed, was in his lunges, wch were not ulcerated neither, but obstructed & opprest wth stiff and clammy matter that he could not voyd ; perspiration was that he wanted, and they supposed a penetrating ayre might doe ye cure ; but that was found too searching & corrasive for the other p̄tes, wch were pervious enough and penetrable ; he, therefore, thought upon Northamptonshire, his native country,

w^{ch}

wch would in reason be most propitious to him ; &, happen what might, he would leave his breath where first he found it, & thankfully returne what had bin serviceable now a long tyme to him.

He had at Preston, fower myles from Heyford, a very deare & bosome friend, that was ambitious of enterteyning good men, one D^r. Dod, & being seriously invited thither, he pitched upon it ; there he enjoyed wth great contentment what ayre, converse wth friends, and loving enterteinment, could afford, and at the first was much refreshed by it ; but, nature being spent, and no foundation left to worke upon, all his refreshing quickly flagged. He had before made use of D^r. Ashworth, a man of much experience, who knew his body well, therefore, he thinkes of riding over unto Oxford to him, and there continued about twelve days, & consulted with such as were there of any note.

Men

Men die and p̄rish when their tyme
is come, as well "errore medici," as " vi
morbi." Dʳ. Ashworth was p̄swaded that
the scorbate was his disease & that yᵉ
London Dʳˢ. had all mistooke their
marke, &, therefore, pitched upon appli-
cations sutable; a great errour for so
experienced & grave a Dʳ.

Desire of restitution into a state of
healthe made shift to flatter Dʳ. Preston into a beleefe that the old man
was right. Dr. Ashworth, upon his
p̄swasion, comes over unto Preston wᵗʰ
him, straines & steepes scurvy grass,
& gives him drenches able to have
weakened a stronger man then he was
now; and having stayed & tampered
wᵗʰ him about three weekes, & finding nothing answer his expectation, he
takes his last leave of him, giving such
order & directions as he thought good,
and so left him & retorned to Oxford, July 9. 1628.

When

When this dreame & fancy of yᵉ scorbate failed, & Dʳ. Ashworth was gone, he resigned up himselfe to God alone, & let all care of physique and Dʳˢ. goe.

He had a servant who had bin laborious wᵗʰ him, & whom he after used as a friend ; he would say, " servi sunt humiles amici ;" as was very true of him. To him he, therefore, now unbossomed himselfe, not only touching yᵉ vanity and emptiness of all thinges heere below, but his owne beleefe & expectation of a suddaine change; "not of my company," said he, "for I shall still converse wᵗʰ God, & saints, but of my place & way of doing it."

He said he should change his place but not his company.

His will was made some yeares before, as I have said ; yet was it doubtfull, when it came to proving, but that it might be bafled & affronted. Therefore, he purposed to wave it, and make a deed of guift to him yᵗ was in that will his
executor,

executor, wth such restrictions & limit-
ations as he thought good ; all wch he
set downe wth his owne hand ; he also
carefully provided for his mother during
life, & both his brothers.   His bookes
& all his furniture & goods belonging to, and in his lodgings at, Emanuel
College, he gave to one of his pupils
that was fellow there, whom he always
greatly favoured.   Some exhibitions he
gave to schollars there, to be disposed
of from tyme to tyme by him that was
executor.   And, as he truly vallued, so
he highly rewarded his servant's faithfulness ; who liveth yet in very good condition & reputation ; of whom is verified
what is said, Prov. 27. 18. "whoso keep-
eth ye figtree shall eate the fruit thereof, so he y^t wayteth on his mast^r shall
surely come to honour."

Having thus discumbred himselfe of
worldly cares, he prayed for his college,
that it might continue a flourishing
nursery

nursery of religion & learning; told
those about him, as David before his
death, 1 Cron. 29. 2. 3. &c., what he
had done towards that goodly building since erected, & what care he had
taken to get those Rectoryes in the
King's L̄r̄e mentioned (whereof I spake
before); prayed God to furnish Lincoln's Inn from time to time wth able
preaching ministers, as also the Lecture-
ship at Cambridge that had cost him
so much trouble in ye procuring; and,
for his sermons, he desired that they
might not come into ye world like
vagabonds, but, seeing the father lived
not to see them setled & provided for,
those would be carefull whom he named.
In all wch great thinges God hath answered him as I thinke no man was since
Elisha, 2 Kings 2. 9. 10.

The night before he dyed, being
Saturday, he went to bedd and lay
about three howers desiring to sleepe,
but

but slept not ; then, said he, " my desolu-
tion is at hand, let me goe to my home
& Jesus Christ who hath bought me
wth his most precious blood," and so
lay still, as in a slumber, till about two
of the clock in the morning ; then drinking, & resting on his servant's armes,
he fell into a cold & clammy sweate,
wch he told them was the messenger
of death, and so continued for about
two howres very sylent ; about fower
of the clock, he said, " I feele death coming to my heart, my paine shall now be
quickly turned into joy ;" and so his
friends were called that were present
in the howse, who spake unto him, but
had no answer from him as they were
used to have. They kneeled all downe
& a Reverend Divine there present
prayed. When prayer was ended D^r.
Preston looked on them, &, turning away
his head, gave up ye Ghost.

It was about 5 of ye clock on the
Lord's

Lord's day, but to him an everlasting
Sabbath ; he never, by his goodwill,
rested that day from preaching since
God was truly knowne unto him, untill
now when God gave him an everlasting rest.

No man deserved better sollemnityes,
but M^r. Dod was much against it ; and
his friends at Cambridge, who did highly
honour him, and desired nothing more
then to have wayted on his dust to his
long home, were now obleiged to attend
the election of another Master ; but they
durst not so much as make it knowne,
or doe any thinge from wch it might be
gathered.   He was buryed decently,
but w^thout state, in Fawley Church, in
the county of Northampton.   Old M^r.
Dod, the minister of that place, preached,
and a world of Godly people came together, July 20. 1628.

Just before his death he asked what
day

day it was, and being answered it was the Sabbath Day, "a fit day," said he, "to be sacrificed on. I have accompanied S^{ts} on earth & now I shall accompany angels in Heaven." Also M^{rs}. Chaderton reminding him of his preaching so profoundly on God's attributes he answered, "if it shall please God to prolong my life, I will make all so plaine, that every one shall be able to understand it."

He was within a little of one-and-forty years of age when he died.

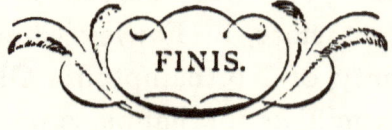

FINIS.

Printed by Parker and Co.,
Crown Yard, Oxford.